Blame It On The Blizzard

Samantha Baca

<u>Sugarplum Falls Series</u>

Blame It On The Mistletoe

Blame It On The Eggnog

Blame It On The Candy Canes

Blame It On The Blizzard

Blame It On The Reindeer

Blame It On The Carols

Blame It On The Lattes

Blame It On The Secret Santa

Cover Design: Richard Baca
Image (s): DepositPhotos

Contents

<u>One</u>
Brynlee

"You've got to be kidding me," I muttered, scrubbing my hand down my face in frustration.

"I'm sorry, dear. It's less than two weeks until Christmas, and we're completely booked." The older woman smiled warmly, but it did nothing to calm the chill snaking its way over my skin. "That storm filled any vacancies we had fast, with so many people getting stuck passing through."

"Are there any other hotels in town that might have a vacancy?" the guy next to me asked, clearly unable to get a room either, as the woman helping him gave him the same sympathetic smile I was given by the woman helping me.

"There's only one other hotel in Sugarplum Falls," the younger woman replied to him. "I can call and check, but Sugarplum Suites is usually completely booked months before the holiday rolls around."

I held my breath, looking up at the sign that read Sugarplum Inn, waiting to see if she had any luck. She held the phone to her ear and greeted whoever was on the other line before frowning and shaking her head no when they confirmed they didn't have any rooms, either.

"Are you sure there's nothing at all?" I asked, desperation thick in my voice. "Not even a linen closet no one uses?"

"I'm sorry, there's nothing available. I've checked everything," she said, pushing her glasses up her nose and leaning closer to her computer to look at it.

I dropped my head.

"All out of rooms?" A burly man questioned, resting a toolbox on the end of the counter.

"Unfortunately. I've never seen this hotel book up so fast in the ten years I've worked here."

His brows pulled together as he frowned and scrubbed his hand along the thick beard that covered his jaw.

"Well, it's not much, but I have a cabin I'm not using if the two of you want it." He looked between me and the guy who went from standing a few feet away from me to being so close that I could smell the soft scent of his cologne.

"We'll take it," he rushed out, not giving me a chance to respond first.

The two men turned their focus to me, waiting.

I looked around, pushing out a frustrated breath as my foot anxiously tapped the tile floor. It wasn't like I had any other options, given that the hotels were full and I couldn't drive to the next town. Who knew if there was even a next town? I had no idea where I was and should consider myself lucky that a kind man was offering me shelter.

But then again, I was always taught never to take anything from a stranger, and one could argue that a cabin might fall under that umbrella. Plus, it wasn't like I knew the guy I would be staying with. That could be incredibly dangerous and was possibly a risk I shouldn't take. Hadn't they seen

20/20? There were plenty of true crime episodes to prove my point that shacking up with a stranger was a terrible idea.

"I'm Sebastian, by the way," the young guy beside me said, extending his hand to the other man while I continued contemplating how many different ways this guy could kill me, chop my body up into tiny pieces, and probably feed it to the reindeer I saw outside when I rushed in.

"I'm Bert. Nice to meet you."

I could feel their attention returning to me again, eyes staring so intently they could probably read my mind.

"I'm a thriller author," I blurted out, pulling my shoulders back squarely.

Sebastian blinked a few times, his lips pressing into a thin line as he tried to keep the smile from forming on his attractive face. I knew my answer startled him; shit, it surprised me too.

"Okay…" He nodded, as if he was trying to see how that was relevant. "Thanks for the info, I guess?" He laughed nervously. "I'm sorry. I'm not sure what to do with that information or what it means."

I narrowed my eyes at him, making myself look more intimidating. I'd seen plenty of shows to know that you were less likely to be captured if you looked like you would be a challenge—or more like a pain in the ass. I wasn't going to let him see an ounce of my fear or uncertainty. No, sir, no way. Fake it til you make it—or, in my case, fake it until you can make it out alive during an insane blizzard being trapped in a cabin with a sexy stranger who might have other plans to murder you two weeks before Christmas.

"It means that I've watched plenty of true crime shows and have done massive amounts of research to know how to kill someone and make it look like an accident," I answered with a raised eyebrow and arms folded over my chest. "And I know how to hide a body or two if needed."

I looked from him to Bert, who quickly raised his hands in front of him, the flannel material of his shirt lifting and showing his round stomach that hung over his jeans.

"Don't tell my wife that. She'll probably take you up on the offer," he teased with a laugh. "Now we'd better get going, or we'll never get up the mountain before that storm blocks the road. I reckon you'll need to stop by the store for reinforcements, so I'll follow you there and then take you up."

"Sounds good. Thank you, Bert," Sebastian said, grabbing his suitcase handle and rolling it out of the way before grabbing mine. "You coming?"

I worried my lower lip between my teeth before looking over at the women at the desk. If I went missing, at least they would be able to say they saw me go with an attractive stranger and would likely be able to give a very accurate description to the sketch artist of what he looked like, given how hard they were staring.

We walked outside, the wind pushing a blast of ice-cold air into our faces as snow swirled by. I lifted my arm to shield it as I tried to catch my breath. Once I got inside my car, everything would be fine. I would be sheltered from the storm and have a few minutes to clear my head.

Only, when I spotted my car, dread filled my stomach when I discovered that the bottom half of it was already submerged in snow as it continued to fall from the sky in record amounts.

"I have a truck," Sebastian offered, noticing my dilemma. "I can help you grab your stuff and give you a ride to the store before we head up to the cabin."

"Thanks," I said tightly, shaking my head as I couldn't believe my luck. I wasn't irritated with him, just that this was happening in general. I grabbed what I could, slightly embarrassed by the amount of baggage I'd brought with me, and helped him load it into the back seat of his truck. Once we were settled, we followed Bert to a store called Waldon's, which was already packed with people rushing to get bottled water and other essentials.

"Want to each take a cart to get what we need and then meet at the registers in twenty minutes?" Sebastian asked once we got inside. Bert had already taken off to grab the things he needed after his wife called.

"Sure. That works." I smiled the friendliest smile I could muster and then pushed the cart away from him, trying to figure out what all I would need. If he was still planning to take me to the cabin and kill me, I wasn't going to give him my best smile—those were reserved for my best friend, Macy.

I squeezed past a handful of people as I tried to make my way down the aisle that everyone else seemed to be focused on. I grew up in southern California, so I had no idea what I would need for a storm of this magnitude. I had already grabbed a case of water from an end cap and then added a few flashlights and some batteries to my cart like the others were before pushing past them.

Bert hadn't said how big the cabin was or whether to expect power there, so I focused on grabbing some canned goods and packets of tuna that didn't require anything other than to open the package and eat it. It wasn't my favorite, but it would do.

I stocked up on crackers and granola bars, looking for things that would work as meal substitutions if needed. I decided against buying anything that required refrigeration and skipped over to the personal care aisle and stocked up on stuff for the bathroom before heading to the clothing section. I had packed what I thought were warm clothes, but after the frigid cold turned my body numb, I decided to grab a few more things.

There were a ton of thermal options, so I grabbed some pajamas and threw them in the cart. I couldn't think of what else was a necessity, so I focused on what would make me feel better with this sudden change of plans. I grabbed a soft throw blanket that was sherpa-lined and added it to my stuff, along with a few boxes of chocolates and some roasted nuts.

By the time I got to the register, Sebastian was already there, checking out. He smiled over his shoulder and then made small talk with the woman ringing him up. Her skin was flushed as she tucked a strand of hair behind her ear, giving him bedroom eyes as she scanned the last item.

I turned my attention to the magazine rack beside me and studied the headlines, debating whether to grab the one who claimed a man had been abducted by aliens in a UFO while sitting on the toilet. My fingers reached for it but quickly moved away as Sebastian approached.

"Did you find everything you needed?" he asked, tucking his receipt into his back pocket.

"I think so. You?" I didn't have the slightest idea what I

needed, so I was pretty confident I had missed something; only time would tell.

"Pretty sure I did. I stocked up on batteries and toilet paper and grabbed a few flashlights in case we needed them. A couple of cases of bottled water. Some protein bars. All of the essentials. I was going to ask what you like to eat so we can plan meals together, but I figured we can talk about that when we get there. I grabbed plenty of food."

"Oh," I mumbled nervously, looking at the items in my cart. "I didn't really buy stuff to—"

"Don't worry about it," he assured me. "Like I said, I grabbed plenty. I have a habit of cooking too much for just one person."

"Thanks," I said softly, looking away as his chocolate-brown eyes studied me.

I lifted my shoulders, hoping the deep breath that I took would fill my lungs. I felt overwhelmed by everything. It was too much.

Never in a million years did I think I would find myself stranded in the middle of nowhere, in some Christmas-obsessed small town, with an incredibly good-looking guy unless I were writing it in some cheesy holiday romance book. But that wasn't my style, which meant it would end up turning into a holiday murder mystery type thriller, which didn't look good for me.

Two
Sebastian

"There's a backup generator, which you'll need once the next storm pushes through. The likelihood of you getting back down the mountain for the foreseeable future is slim. I've gone ahead and put my extra first aid kit in the bathroom in case you guys need it. There's a pantry in the kitchen where you can store your stuff. I haven't been up here in a while, so I doubt there's much in it. Feel free to help yourself to whatever you need. And there's firewood in the detached garage, but you may need to chop more before the storm passes. You know how to do that?" Bert asked as he studied me with arms folded over his chest.

"Yes, sir. My grandpa taught me when I was younger. I haven't been through a storm of this magnitude before, but I'm familiar with the weather in Montana."

"Good. You'll be fine then. There's space in the garage for you to bring it in and cut it there. I've got my set up in the corner; you'll see it when you go in. Leave the wet wood out to dry and stay ahead of it so you don't run short."

"Will do," I promised.

"There's also Christmas decorations up on the rafters in there. There are some lights and a small tree that will look nice in that corner. That's where my wife Janice always insists on putting it when we come up. You don't have to go crazy with the decorations, but there are a lot to choose from.”

“Okay. Sounds good.” I smiled but wasn’t sure what else to say.

“Christmas is a big thing around Sugarplum Falls,” Bert said, rocking back on his heels as he shoved his hands in his coat pockets. “Everyone around town makes a big deal of it and decorates for the holiday. This cabin is still in Sugarplum Falls, even if it’s way up here. My friend Sam always says there’s nothing a little Christmas spirit can’t solve, and if that fails, then eat a candy cane or two. Now, that’s not the real saying, but it’ll have to do.” Bert nodded to both of us and then turned on his heel to leave. “If you need anything, my phone number is written on the board on the fridge.”

He nodded and looked around as if he was trying to see if there was something he was forgetting to tell us, like the fact that the cabin was tiny and barely fit one full-sized bed and a few chairs in what was supposed to be considered the living room area.

“Alright, well, I guess you two are all set. Sorry it’s not the best, but it’ll keep you from losing a toe trying to sleep in your truck.”

“We appreciate your generosity,” I said, shaking his hand. “Thank you for allowing us to stay here.”

Bert had already declined any payment for us using the cabin, but I was determined to find a way to pay him back regardless.

We gave each other a final nod before he stepped outside and hurried to his truck while I pushed against the wind to get the door shut. Once secured, I locked it and slid the deadbolt up top into place.

I turned around to find the beautiful woman with long dark hair and large green eyes scanning the room as she sat in one of the chairs, knees tucked into her chest.

"I'm Sebastian," I said cautiously as I approached and sat in the other chair.

"I know. You told me." She lowered her chin and watched me.

"Yeah, but you haven't told me your name yet."

She chewed her lip nervously as she watched me. She had acted tough earlier when she told me she was a thriller author and assured me she knew plenty of ways to murder me and hide the body. But now, she seemed scared and vulnerable, which pulled at my heart in a way I hadn't expected.

"Why do you want to know it?" she questioned.

I lifted my hands and let them fall as I leaned back into the recliner, spreading my legs out in front of me.

"I guess it just sounds better than saying *hey, you* all the time."

A tense silence filled the air for a few minutes before she tilted her head and looked at me.

"Brynlee. Brynlee Marie Adams. I'm twenty-eight. I graduated with honors. I had an imaginary pet when I was little, a dog named Pebbles. She was a cocker spaniel and my only friend because I was in and out of foster care homes and never in one place long enough to build a lasting friendship. I was a book nerd throughout high school and was never one of the popular kids."

"Wow. Okay," I said with a soft laugh, soaking all of the information up. "I wasn't expecting that, but thank you."

Her green eyes blinked a few times before her shoulders relaxed slightly.

"It's proven that killers are less likely to kill their victims if they feel they know them and have a personal connection to them. Now you know something about me. Personal details." She jutted her chin out, but the way her breathing changed, I questioned how much of it was true.

"First—I have no plans to kill you. Second, I don't think that's 100% true. Look at the rate of people killing their spouses, parents, or children. They know them personally and still kill them."

"Anyone can kill anyone," she sighed as if I were the stupidest person on the planet. "Men are far more likely to target a stranger and stalk their victim. They enjoy the chase of going after someone vulnerable. Women are more likely to target someone familiar to them—usually a spouse or partner." She lifted her eyebrows as if to drive her point across.

"So, because I'm a man, I'm supposed to be a cold-hearted killer? You do realize that I wasn't stalking you, right? We both ended up at this cabin because we got stuck in a crazy blizzard with nowhere to go. This wasn't premeditated."

"So you say," she said with a shrug. "I couldn't see much in that storm, so who knows how long you might have been following me."

I shoved a hand through my short hair and stared at her in disbelief.

"Alright, but what if this is a deeper plot, and instead of being the predictable villain and storyline, we throw everyone for a loop? Who's to say that you're not some obsessed fan of mine who *stalked me*, lured *me* to this cabin, and now plans to *murder me* because you're in love with me?" I challenged, leaning forward and resting my elbows on my knees.

"That's easy," she said with a soft snort and shake of her head. "I don't even know who you are."

We stared at each other for a few minutes, neither looking away.

"So, you're telling me you haven't heard of F.E. Tish?"

Her mouth opened briefly to say something but quickly snapped shut. Her cheeks tinted the cutest shade of pink as she adjusted in her seat, pulling her knees closer to her chest.

"So you *do* know who I am," I teased.

"I didn't know who you were," she insisted quickly. "Like everyone, I assumed F.E. Tish was a woman. It's not like there are images of the author floating around the internet."

"Nope," I replied, letting the *p* at the end pop.

"So I'm stuck in a cabin with a New York Times bestselling author of erotic romance, *who* also just happens to be a male working under a pen name and highly likely to murder me and feed my body to the reindeer in Sugarplum Falls. Lovely."

"Trust me," I said as I got up from the chair. "You don't have to worry about me killing you. While I also do plenty of research for my writing, none of it revolves around how to kill someone and get away with it. If anything, I should be worried about *you*."

I turned and headed to the bathroom, giving her a moment to soak that in while I took one to clear my head.

14

Three

Brynlee

Five. Six. Seven. Eight. Nine. Ten.

I slowly released the deep breath I was holding and forced my shoulders down from my ears. Sebastian was still in the bathroom while I stared at the only bed in the cabin that we would be forced to share. Unless one of us was willing to sleep upright in one of the clunky, uncomfortable-looking chairs, there were no other options. The floor would be hard and cold, but not only that, there was barely any room between the pieces of furniture for someone to lie down comfortably.

My head was still spinning that he just so happened to be one of my favorite authors—more so that *he* wasn't a *she,* as I thought. I had been reading F.E. Tish's books since they came out a few years ago and devoured them. Not only were they super steamy, but the plot was always so well developed that I could get lost in the story, with the spicy sex scenes being a bonus.

I would be lying if I said I didn't get imposter syndrome every time I tried to write after reading an F.E. Tish book. But now I was stuck in a cabin with F.E. Tish, and thoughts about how he came up with those wild sex scenes invaded my mind. *Did he have a girlfriend he practiced them with?*

"Everything okay?" he asked, standing beside the bed, startling me.

I had been so lost in thought that I hadn't heard him come back.

"Oh. Yeah. Everything is fine."

I shook my head to clear some of the intrusive thoughts as his eyes watched me.

If readers knew that F.E. Tish was this attractive, they would lose their minds. That was probably why I never saw his name listed at any book signings.

I could picture him sitting there, shoving a hand through his dark, tousled hair as he smiled a perfect smile, driving all the women mad. He would lick his plump lips, drawing their attention as they imagined everything they wanted that mouth of his to do them. Then he would stand up and stretch, his fitted sweater lifting just enough to reveal smooth skin and deep v-lines that cut deep into his perfectly sculpted muscles. They would be itching to get their hands on him, to see if he was the full package—in every way imaginable.

"Ahem. Brynlee?" He cleared his throat loudly.

My head whipped up to look at him, my eyes blinking rapidly as I tried to get that delicious image out of my head.

"Sorry?" I pulled my brows together in confusion.

"Are you sure you're okay?" There was a hint of humor in his tone as he sat on the edge of the bed and folded his hands in his lap.

I quickly averted my eyes, trying *not* to look at his crotch, just in case the little one-eyed monster wanted to greet me with a standing ovation.

"Yeah. Why wouldn't I be?"

I could feel the heat rising through my veins as I struggled to regulate my breathing.

"I don't know," he said easily, pulling his lower lip between his teeth before releasing it. "You're blushing quite a bit for someone who was in here by herself. I'm kinda curious about what you were thinking about."

I swallowed hard, trying to get past the lump in my throat.

"I'm not blushing," I lied, tucking a strand of hair behind my ear.

"Oh, sorry. I must have been mistaken." He stood up and winked at me, sending a jolt right through me.

"I'm going to make something for dinner. You hungry?" he asked from the kitchen, which was technically still the same room, given that the bathroom was the only thing not in there.

He opened the refrigerator, bending slightly at the waist as he grabbed stuff and set it on the counter.

"Steak and potatoes good for you?" he questioned when I still hadn't given him an answer.

"Tuna," I blurted out, my cheeks flaming with embarrassment as he turned and arched an eyebrow.

I went from worrying that he was a serial killer, ready to cut me up and feed me to the reindeer, to being completely awkward now that I knew who he was.

But just because he was a New York Times bestselling author who I *loved* didn't mean that deep down he wasn't a sadistic killer. Everyone had their faults, even Sebastian, AKA F.E. Tish.

"I bought tuna," I clarified, clearing my throat. "I'll have that for dinner."

I lowered my head and looked away from him as he opened and closed cabinet doors until he found the one with pots and pans.

"I bought plenty of food, Brynlee. I enjoy cooking and would love to make you dinner if you'd allow me to."

I opened my mouth to say something but stopped when I thought better of it.

"And no, it's not so I can get you to trust me before I murder you. Look it up and I'm sure you'll find that most serial killers don't bother cooking elaborate meals for their victims."

I grabbed my phone from my pocket and started typing. I heard a low chuckle as he turned to the counter and started working on dinner.

Instead of Googling whether serial killers cook for their victims, I sent a quick text message to my best friend to let her know what was happening. I was surprised to find that there was decent Wi-Fi at the cabin and that I hadn't lost reception yet.

Me: If I die, tell the police I was stranded in a cabin in Sugarplum Falls with F.E. Tish. SHE is really a HE who writes under a pen name. Real name is Sebastian. I don't know his last name. He's trying to cook for me— likely so he can poison me. It'll be faster that way.

Me: He's incredibly good-looking. 6'2-6'3. Slender but very muscular. Short brown hair. Dark brown eyes. Thin stubble of hair on his face in a perfectly trimmed goatee.

Macy: I'm glad you made it somewhere safe. Send me your location, and I'll save it.

Macy: You're with F.E. TISH!!! OH MY GOD!!

Macy: She is a he?! And smoking hot!! You're so freaking lucky!!!

Macy: He is not going to kill you. By the sounds of it, you're more likely to die from too many orgasms than from food poisoning.

I looked up from my phone to find him opening a seasoning packet and sprinkling it on the steaks he'd put in a glass baking dish.

Me: THAT'S where everyone gets things wrong—they trust the attractive guy because he looks TOO good-looking to be a killer. Then BAM—I'm dead. And I can't even come back to say I told you so.

Macy: I've said it before, and I'll say it again—you need to watch a little less true crime and a little more porn. Relax and enjoy your time there.

Me: I'm not going to watch porn.

Macy: Why not?

Me: Because I'm not like that. I don't need to watch people having sex. It's so gross.

Macy: But watching in detail how someone murdered a human being and hearing all the gruesome details isn't?

Me: No, it's calming.

Macy: I'm just saying you can relax a little. Not

everyone is out to kill you. Keep me posted on how things are going there. Are you going to be able to work?

Me: I hope so. There seems to be decent Wi-Fi so far. There's a table and chairs so I don't need much more than that. I have my laptop so I can binge some shows there if I need inspiration.

Macy: When do you have to submit your manuscript?

Me: Ten days.

Macy: Christmas Eve?

Me: Yup. Merry Christmas to me if I don't get this done on time.

Macy: You will. You've got this.

Me: (heart emoji)

Macy: (heart emoji)

Macy: Call me if you need anything. Otherwise, try to enjoy your time.

I tucked my phone back into my pocket and squared my shoulders before heading into the kitchen.

"So, what did Google say?" Sebastian asked with a cocky grin over his shoulder.

"I didn't Google anything," I admitted, digging through my bags of groceries to find the tuna. "I was texting my best friend."

"Did you tell her about me?"

"Yes. I gave her a good description of you in case she

needed to report anything to the authorities. I would have sent a picture, but I didn't have one." I looked up to find his eyes on mine.

"If you want a picture, all you have to do is ask."

I raised my eyebrows, hearing the hint of flirting laced through his words.

"How about a selfie?" he asked, wiping his hands on a towel and stepping toward me.

"Nope," I shook my head, holding my hand up.

He stopped abruptly, the corners of his lips lifting.

"No? I thought one of my biggest fans would want a picture now that they knew who I was," he teased, folding his arms over his chest.

"I never said I was a fan," I corrected, grabbing my phone. "And I'm not taking a selfie with you."

"Why not?"

"Because then the police would see it, and it would look like we were friendly with each other, which would help rule you out as a suspect. I'm already onto you." I lifted my phone and snapped a photo, pressing the button to send it to Macy.

He blinked a few times as if he wasn't sure what just happened.

"I'm totally onto you," he said, cocking his head to the side.

"Onto me?" I screeched. "*I'm* not the one who uses a fake name and is likely to be a cold-blooded killer."

"Why do I have to be a cold-blooded killer?"

"Because you're all good-looking and mysterious, trying to get me to lower my walls to trust you. You have killer written all over you."

"I'll tell you a little secret," he said, his dark eyes gleaming in the light.

He curled his finger for me to come closer. I stood where I was and let him come to me. He leaned in to whisper in my ear, his scent captivating my senses again.

"The only time I've been called a killer was in the bedroom after I gave her seven orgasms. But don't worry, I won't tell anyone why you really wanted that picture of me."
He winked, making sure I was picking up on what he was implying.

He pulled away and got back to dinner while I stood there with my jaw hanging open.

Four
Sebastian

Dinner went surprisingly well, given that Brynlee sat with her steak knife tucked into the side of her plate the entire time as if she was afraid she would need to use it at any given moment. I tried to make conversation, but it was hard with her still putting up walls every time. I knew she still felt uneasy being in the cabin with someone she didn't know, so I took my victory in getting her to eat the dinner I made instead of her tuna packet.

"I'll do the dishes," I offered as we cleared our plates and took them to the sink.

"Is that so you can make sure you get all of the fingerprints off yours first?" she asked, but there was a spark of humor in her eyes for once.

"You really don't trust me, do you?" I shook my head with a grin plastered across my face.

I understood how unnerving it had to be to be forced into staying with a complete stranger, but I wished I could make her see that I would never in a million years ever think of hurting her. The only time I would ever consider hurting someone was if it was in self-defense or to protect another.

"I don't know you," she replied with a shrug as she squirted some soap onto a washrag and began cleaning her plate.

"What do you want to know?" I asked, stepping beside her with a towel to dry the dishes. "I'm an open book."

Apparently, she was going to help whether I wanted her to or not.

"I find it odd that you're an open book, yet you write under a pen name," she said softly, looking up at me under dark lashes.

 "When I wrote my first book, my agent advised me to write it under a pen name. She said it would do better if people thought a woman wrote it. So we launched it under F.E. Tish, and things just skyrocketed from there," I answered, setting the clean plate on the counter as she washed mine.

"How did you come up with your pen name?"

"It's going to sound childish, but I couldn't think of anything original. Everything my agent proposed sounded like I was an eighty-year-old woman who wanted to talk about burning loins. I couldn't get on board with that and wanted something different. Something that gave me the ability to write what I wanted to."

"Does F.E. Tish have a special meaning to it? Is it someone's initials?" she questioned, lowering her head as she focused on the dishes.

"Nope. It's actually just the word fetish broken up. F. E. Tish. Nothing special, but I felt like it represented what I wrote, given my books tend to involve fetishes and embracing your sexuality."

"The complete opposite of an eighty-year-old woman with burning loins," she teased with a soft laugh. I loved the sound of it and wondered how I could get more out of her.

"Definitely," I laughed. "So, what about you? What got you into writing thrillers?"

She inhaled deeply, letting it slowly flow through her lips before answering.

"I've always loved horror, and growing up, I couldn't get enough of Stephen King. I would reread his books when I ran out of stuff to read. It always fascinated me, and I felt this longing to write one of my own, so I went for it."

"How long have you been published?"

"My debut novel was released a little over a year ago. Since then, I have released one more, and the one I'm working on will be book three in the series. There will be six total."

Her cheeks flushed the prettiest shade of pink as she looked away again, this time to grab our glasses from the counter beside her.

"Congratulations. That's an amazing accomplishment."

"Thank you. It's not quite as big as yours."

"Size doesn't always matter," I joked before I could stop myself.

She turned and looked at me with a shocked expression before she burst into laughter. A soap-covered hand flew out of the water to cover her mouth as she laughed.

"I don't think I've ever heard a guy admit that before," she said, giggles still coming from her lips.

"Well, it's true. And a lot of guys wouldn't admit half the

stuff I would." I shrugged, knowing her curiosity was now piquing.

"Oh yeah? Like what?"

Now, I had her right where I wanted her.

"Hmmm," I said, thinking about what would actually impress her. "I'm also an only child. I didn't have any pets, but I always thought I would be that guy who had a cool pet—like a boa constrictor or iguana. I was the popular kid in school but always felt lonely because no one ever took the time to get to know me. The only thing they cared about was others thinking they were cool because they hung out with me. Christmas is my favorite holiday. And I cried during *Love Actually* when he brings the sign to declare his love for her, even though she's married to his best friend."

She turned off the water to face me, studying me carefully.

"You told me a lot of personal stuff when you thought I was a serial killer, so I thought I would start there," I replied with a shrug.

"I'm sorry you were lonely growing up."

"Thanks. It's okay. Things turned out the way they were supposed to. Very few people know my pen name, which helps keep my relationships real instead of people wanting to be *friends with a bestselling author*."

"Well, my friend knows it now," she said, scrunching her face. "I told her your real name and sent a picture. But she won't tell anyone, I promise. It was just in case you, you know…"

"Killed you?" I offered with a grin.

"I'm sorry. I shouldn't have told her. I didn't know you kept it that much of a secret."

"It's alright. It's hard enough to keep it a secret as it is. My agent wants me to consider doing some book signings and press releases when the next series starts, but I haven't decided yet. But eventually, people will know who I am."

"Your fans love you. I'm sure they'll be pleasantly surprised to see you're a man, not a woman."

"But not you, right?" I teased. "You're not one of those fans?"

She eyed me cautiously as she pulled her lower lip between her teeth.

"I'm undecided."

"Fair enough." I laughed, stacking the rest of the dishes on the counter to put them away.

"I mean, I think the thing that really gets me is that you cried during *Love Actually*."

I turned around and faced her head on, my grin spreading across my cheeks.

"Have you seen it?"

She shook her head.

"No, but friends have told me about it. But I mean, there had to be a better solution than him just writing her a note and wasting all of those cards."

"Okay, I'll bite. What would you have done differently?" I asked, leaning my hip against the counter.

"That's easy. I would have had him kill the best friend so he could be with her. If they were truly meant to be together, then remove the obstacle."

My eyebrows shot up my forehead.

"What?" She laughed. "What would you have done, Mr. Romance Author?"

"I would have kept his friend alive—dear Lord, Brynlee, it's a *Christmas* movie!"

"Yeah, but if the friend is in the way, you have to deal with it. Otherwise, they can't be together and have their *happily ever after*." She lifted her fingers to do air quotes.

"Sure they can." I folded my arms over my chest, loving that she was finally engaging with me.

"Okay, how?"

"Easy—they all end up together."

"Like a threesome?"

"Or a throuple."

Her brows pinched together.

"It's when three people are in a committed relationship. They all unanimously agree to be in a romantic, loving relationship together with the consent of everyone involved. So yeah, they could be together without having to kill off the friend since they both technically love him, too."

"We live in two very different worlds," she muttered jokingly with a grin.

<u>Five</u>
Brynlee

"How do you want to do this?" he asked, standing there in a pair of low-hung grey joggers distracting me.

"Do what?" I tried to focus, but it was impossible. It was like I knew what was lurking beneath the layers of tightly knit cotton, taunting me…

"Sleep together, Brynlee," he said with a chuckle, shifting his weight.

I swallowed hard, his words finally making their way to my brain.

Sleep together? Wasn't that a bit presumptuous to assume we would just jump into bed together the first night? I mean, he was attractive—there was no doubt about that. Did he really find me attractive, or was this his way of throwing me off enough to let my guard down so he could move in for the kill?

"Brynlee?" he asked, clearly struggling to keep the humor out of his voice.

"Yeah?" I looked up and blinked a few times, trying to get his face into focus. I still couldn't believe I was stranded here with F.E. Tish, discussing whether to sleep with the guy who had *warmed up* many of my lonely nights with the words he'd written.

"You okay?"

"Yeah. Absolutely," I stammered. "Why wouldn't I be?"

If we slept together, would he be as gifted as the heroes he wrote about? Would I see stars as my toes curled from mind-blowing orgasms? Would his dirty words be the thing that sent me over the edge, or would it be the way his skilled fingers trailed over my skin?

"You just seem a little *flustered*."

Shit. Was I that obvious?

I knew my cheeks were flushed and I was struggling to keep from looking at his crotch, but I hadn't expected him to notice. He folded his arms over his chest, studying me as I rushed to think of something. My eyes refused to follow simple commands and stayed glued to his groin, earning a soft chuckle from him.

"Serial killers often lack empathy and guilt," I blurted out, a bead of sweat dotting my brow. It was a stupid thing to say, but it was the easiest way to detract from the flush in my cheeks from the dirty thoughts I had been having of him.

I looked up to find his eyebrows lifted as a cheeky grin spread across his face.

"Well, I can assure you that I'm very empathetic. And again, I have no plans to murder you, Brynlee."

I nodded as if it were a sufficient answer, even though there wasn't an actual question attached.

"So, what did you decide?" he asked.

"About what?" My voice hitched in the back of my throat. I still couldn't get my focus back.

"Sleeping together."

"Oh. Um." I tugged nervously at the bottom of my t-shirt, pulling it down over the sleep pants I had changed into. "You're a very attractive guy, and I'm sure you know what you're doing in bed. I mean, you've admitted to researching stuff for your books—which I've read, and they're hot. Like really hot." I stopped for a moment and discreetly fanned my shirt against my skin to cool me off, suddenly regretting putting on the thermal pajamas. "But I don't know that we should just jump right in and have sex with each other."

Did I seriously just say that? How was I standing there talking about sex with F.E. Tish?!

I looked up to find his brown eyes lit up as he found humor in this.

"What?" I laughed nervously. "I know you're probably used to women just throwing their panties at you and giving in to your every command, but I'm not like that. I don't just jump into bed with men I don't know."

His tongue swiped across his plump lower lip, drawing my attention to it.

"I wasn't asking you to have sex with me," he said confidently, tilting his head to the side. "I was asking how you wanted to share the bed since there's only one. I would offer to sleep on the floor or in a chair, but neither of those seem to be an option."

He was right. The room was small, and most of the furniture was piled on top of each other, leaving minimal room to walk while making everything functional. There wouldn't be enough space for either of us to sleep on the floor, and from the looks of the worn wood floors, it wouldn't be comfortable either.

I closed my eyes and took a deep, calming breath. I needed to get it together and fast.

"I'm sorry. I don't know what's wrong with me," I said, pinching the bridge of my nose as I closed my eyes.

"You were forced to share a cabin with someone you don't know during the middle of a record-breaking blizzard in a small town you've never been to. It's okay to be nervous and guarded. I would judge you more if you weren't."

"And yet you're so calm about it," I teased softly, feeling some of the tension ease from my shoulders.

He shrugged his shoulder and shoved his hands into his pockets.

"It's different being a guy and being stuck in this situation than it is being a girl. I may not watch as much true crime as you do, but I've seen enough to know why this situation would make anyone uncomfortable. I could tell you until I'm blue in the face that you don't have anything to worry about with me, but I would rather you find that out yourself. Having you trust me isn't something that I take lightly, so again, are you sure you're comfortable sharing the bed?"

"You're right. There aren't any other options," I agreed, holding my shoulders back to appear as relaxed as possible.

"I can sleep in the tub," he offered, his lips curling up into a smile. "You'd just have to wake me if you need the restroom so I can get out and give you privacy."

"You're not sleeping in the tub," I replied with a soft laugh. It was the first time tonight that I had felt light about something. "We'll share the bed. There are plenty of blankets that we can use to stay warm while also creating a divider between us."

"Okay. If you're sure."

"I am." I nodded and took a calming breath as he grabbed blankets from the closet.

34

<u>Six</u>
Sebastian

I was finishing my shower when the smell of coffee floated underneath the door and grabbed hold of my senses. I rinsed quickly, then shut the water off so there would be plenty of hot water left for Brynlee since she was already up. I pulled on a clean hoodie and a fresh pair of joggers and grabbed my dirty clothes. Brynlee stood at the counter, watching the snow fall out the window as the coffee brewed beside her.

"Good morning," I said, surprisingly chipper, given how tired I was from not sleeping well last night.

"Good morning." She looked over her shoulder, her green eyes catching in the light. "I'm making coffee if you want some."

"Thank you. I would love a cup."

I set my dirty clothes beside my suitcase, ensuring everything was out of the way before heading to the kitchen.

"How did you sleep?" I asked, filling my cup after she filled hers.

"Not great. I think I got an hour, maybe two at most. You?"

"Same." I leaned against the counter and lifted the cup to my lips as she took a sip of hers.

"It sucks. I really needed last night to be a good night's sleep," she grumbled softly, looking out the window again. "I'm never going to make my deadline at this rate."

"For a book?"

She nodded but didn't look at me.

"I'm up against a tight deadline, too. When is yours?"

"Christmas Eve." She sighed and pulled her lips into a thin line as she looked my way. "You?"

"New Year's Eve."

"Are you close to finishing?" she asked, taking another sip.

I shook my head and let a grin tug at my lips.

"I haven't even started."

Her eyes widened with surprise.

"How long is it supposed to be?"

"Full length, which for me is around 80-90,000 words."

She set her cup down and pulled her phone from her hoodie pocket, her fingers moving quickly across the screen.

"It's already the 15th," she said in disbelief. "You have less than three weeks to write an entire book?"

"Yup."

She blinked several times.

"I don't know how you can write so fast. It takes me at least a month to plot a book, then easily four to five to write the first draft."

"I can usually crank books out pretty fast, but even this is pushing it for me."

"Why did you wait so long to get started?" she asked, lifting her cup back to her lips.

"I don't know," I sighed, scrubbing a hand down my face. "I tried starting it months ago but couldn't get it going. Nothing I tried worked. I was struggling to find any creativity and felt like I was being smothered. My girlfriend broke up with me three days ago, and I decided that was it."

"That was the motivation to get you to start writing?" she asked, tilting her head to the side.

"No, that was the motivation to take my life back."

She pulled her brows together and listened.

"Mary Jane was like a wet cloth wrapped tightly around my face, smothering and keeping me from breathing. It was one of those relationships where you get so comfortable with being in one and don't realize that neither of you is getting what you need. But we were both too busy with work to see that. When she broke up with me, I felt relieved. I packed my shit, got in my truck, and just left."

"Where were you going?"

"I don't know," I laughed. "I had no fucking clue. I just threw my belongings in my truck and got the hell out of there. I ended up on the highway with my past getting smaller in the rearview mirror as my future suddenly became brighter."

"Wow," she said softly. "That's quite the inspiring story."

I scrunched my face in response.

"Not really. I didn't get too far before that blizzard hit, and I got stranded here. In my mind, I was going to go as far as the road would take me, living my life without being held back or tied down to anything. I planned to stay in hotels or rent a cabin by the lake where I could write and not have to answer to anyone."

"Well, technically, you're still in a cabin. However, I don't know if there's a lake anywhere near here. I should probably look that up—you know, just in case you decide to go all *Jack Torrance* on me," she teased.

"Who?"

"You know—Jack? Here's Johnny?" She raised her eyebrows and waited. "From *The Shining*?"

"Haven't watched it," I admitted.

"Come to think of it, you kinda remind me of him," she said, narrowing her eyes as she pointed a finger at me. "He was a writer too. Wanted some peace and quiet to get his book done…"

"You're kidding, right?"

"I don't joke when it comes to horror novels," she said with so much seriousness.

"Well, good to know. But on that note, I'm going to make some breakfast to get the day started. You want some eggs?"

"I already ate, but thank you." She glanced at the box of granola bars on the counter.

"That's not breakfast."

"Yes, it is." She laughed, giving me a puzzled look. "That's what I always eat for breakfast."

"You need more brain fuel than that, especially if you're going to crank out some words today. How do you like your eggs?" I asked, ignoring her objections as I set my cup on the counter and opened the fridge. I was glad we hadn't lost power, and from the looks of it outside, we might catch a break after all now that the wind had calmed down some.

"You don't have to make me breakfast," she insisted with a hand on her hip. "I'm fine."

I closed the refrigerator door and turned to face her with folded arms.

"You and I both know that you're going to struggle with writing today if you don't have the energy you need. Given that we both slept like shit last night, we're going to need all the fuel we can get. We already have coffee, so why don't you tell me how you like your eggs so I can make us breakfast and we can get our day started?"

"What if I don't like eggs?" she countered, taking a step closer and jutting her chin.

"Then I'll make something else. What do you want?"

I knew she was trying to make herself appear tough and independent, but she was so damn adorable that I wanted to bottle her up in a little snow globe and keep her forever. And that had nothing to do with the fact that I kind of wanted to shake her for being so difficult over food.

She sighed heavily, her shoulders sagging as she gave up.

"Eggs are fine, thank you. But I'll help you cook."

"I've got it," I assured her.

"You cooked dinner for me last night. And now you're

insisting on making me breakfast. The least I can do is help."

"I don't think it takes two people to make eggs," I teased. "If you want to be helpful, you can… I don't know. Umm… tell me about the worst date you've ever had?"

I grabbed the pan and put it on the burner as she watched me.

"Why would I do that?"

"For research. I need a terrible date story, and I'm drawing blanks."

"Because you're such a great dater you've never had a bad one?"

I could hear the teasing in her tone and loved it. At least she wasn't going on about how she thought I would kill her anymore.

"No, I just don't date."

"What?"

"It's true," I said, rubbing a slice of butter into the pan as it melted quickly against the heat. I grabbed an egg, cracked it, and slowly poured it into the pan.

"What about your girlfriend?"

"*Ex*," I corrected.

"Okay, what about your *ex*-girlfriend? Didn't you guys date?"

"Not really. I met her at the coffee shop where I used to go to write. We spent so much time together there that we kinda just fell into a relationship."

"How long were you together?"

"A year? I don't really remember. Time just started blurring together, and before I knew it, we were living together and in a relationship."

"Wow."

"Yeah." I sighed, moving the eggs with the spatula. "I dated more in my early twenties, but once I entered my thirties, I just got tired of all the bullshit and games that came with trying to get to know someone. Then Mary Jane came along, and it felt easy. Probably because neither of us was in love, but it was nice having someone to go home to most of the time."

"Well, I'm twenty-eight and don't date, so I can't help you either," she said almost wistfully.

"No boyfriend back home?" I asked, passing a glance at her over my shoulder.

"Nope. I like my space. My routines. I don't like having to justify why I like watching the stuff I do or why I write what I write. It's not too surprising that men aren't typically attracted to a woman who has researched a hundred different ways to kill someone and make it look like an accident."

"It wouldn't bother me," I said before I could stop myself. I ignored the heat from her gaze as it penetrated the back of my head while I flipped the eggs.

"You say that now, but I've seen the look that crosses your face when I mention random facts about serial killers."

I removed the eggs from the heat and started the next batch. I had no idea how many she would eat, but I enjoyed talking with her and didn't want it to stop.

"I think anyone might look that way, given the topic," I teased. "Just like if I started spouting off random facts about the stuff I research, I would surely get the same reaction—or worse—from you."

"I doubt it. I have pretty thick skin. Not much bothers me. I can watch true crime shows while eating dinner and not even flinch when they show the graphic stuff."

I cracked the last egg into the skillet and tossed the shell into the trash.

"That's not the kind of stuff I research," I said evenly, leaning against the counter as my eyes locked onto hers.

"What do you research?" she asked, her voice quieter than a few minutes ago.

"We'll just say that I watch a lot of porn." I winked and turned around to tend to the eggs while I let that simmer.

Seven
Brynlee

"Ugh," I groaned, stretching my arms over my head.

Sebastian arched an eyebrow and looked at me over his laptop. We had decided to share the space at the table, with each of us taking a side so we could both work on our manuscripts.

At first, I had been opposed to it because I didn't think there was a chance in hell that I could focus on what I needed to write with his fingers drumming away on his keyboard. But surprisingly, it didn't bother me at all. Instead, it was almost like being in a race against him to see who could get the most words written.

"Break time?" he asked, leaning away from his computer.

I nodded and stood up, my body already aching from sitting in an uncomfortable chair for so long.

"I'm going to head outside for some fresh air. Wanna join?"

I glanced out the floor-to-ceiling window, staring at the snow. It had stopped for the most part, and the wind had died down, so maybe it wouldn't be too bad. We hadn't even been stuck in the cabin for 48 hours, and I was already feeling stir-crazy from the confined space.

"Sure." I grabbed my coat from behind the door and slid on my boots while Sebastian grabbed his.

Once we stepped outside, a blast of frigid cold air whipped us in the face, taking my breath away. I covered my mouth with a gloved hand and turned in the opposite direction. Maybe it was a bit windier than I had thought.

Sebastian jerked his head to the side as he tightened the scarf around his neck, bringing it up slightly to cover his face. I followed him around the side of the house and let out a breath of relief when we stepped onto a covered porch off the back. There were two brick walls that supported a sturdy overhang and a concrete bench that was covered in snow. But other than that, it was mostly shielded from the storm and a safe place to sit.

I wiped my arm across the bench, clearing the majority of the snow before sitting down. It was colder than I anticipated, but being out of the cabin for a few minutes felt nice.

"Sorry, I didn't expect it to be *this* cold out here," he said loudly behind a gloved hand as he sat down beside me. "The sun was misleading."

"It's okay. I needed to get out of the cabin for a few minutes. I was starting to feel claustrophobic."

"Me too."

"At least it's not as windy back here," I offered, looking around at the space.

He nodded and rubbed his hands together.

"My ass is already frozen." He shifted slightly as if trying to unfreeze it.

"Mine too. I can't feel it anymore."

We both laughed and kept rubbing our hands together to stay warm.

"So, how's it going with your manuscript?" he asked, looking at me.

"Good, I guess. I've written myself into a hole, so now I have to figure out how to get myself out. You?"

"Same. I thought I knew what direction I was going, but now that I'm there, I don't like where it's heading."

I lowered my head and studied the patterns in the snow on the ground from where the wind had blown it.

"So, what's your problem? Maybe I can help?" he offered.

"My FBI agent is trying to track down the man who set her up and framed her for her partner's murder, but this other guy keeps popping up and getting in the way. I haven't figured out what to do with him yet."

"That's easy," he replied confidently. "He's her love interest. Have him help her solve the case, and then they can live happily ever after."

I pinched my brows together and shook my head.

"No. It doesn't work that way."

"Why not?"

"Because people don't fall in love in my books. She doesn't have time for a love interest. She has a case to solve before the person trying to kill her finds her. She's strong. Independent. She doesn't need a man to do this for her."

He shrugged and thought about it.

"Why can't she be strong and still accept his help? Why is love a bad thing?"

"Because people get stupid when love is involved. They get sloppy. Make mistakes. She doesn't have the luxury of allowing that to happen. Her life depends on it, and if she stops for a moment to be enamored by some incredibly good-looking guy who has the potential to sweep her off her feet, that'll be the end of her."

He chuckled lightly, clearly entertained by this.

"Of her or you?" he teased softly.

"Both. If she dies, I die. This is book three in a six-book series, and we've made it this far without love getting in the way. I don't think my agent is going to be pleased when I turn this series into a romance when everyone is counting on me slicing and dicing people instead."

"Alright. Fair enough." He rubbed his hands together quickly, thinking it through.

"I've got it."

"You do?" I looked up at him under my lashes, digging the excitement in his eyes.

"Yup, and you're going to love it."

"Alright, let's hear it."

"So, he comes into the picture as the nice guy, the one who is going to help her figure things out. As they start to get closer, she gets this feeling deep inside that something more sinister is going on. Instead of him being the good guy, he's actually the villain and leading the whole thing. Only by the time she realizes it, it's too late, and he has her right where he wants her."

I leaned back against the wall behind me and thought about

it. It wasn't terrible and could work if I moved a few things around.

"That's actually not bad," I admitted, letting my hair fall to the side as I turned my head to look at him.

"Thanks. It was fun to play it all out in my head. Do you think it could work?"

"Possibly. I already had a villain lined up, but now that I think about it, it was probably a dead giveaway from the start. This will be a good twist my readers won't see coming."

"Especially if you have him help her get to the 'bad guy.' Then, when she thinks he's going to help her capture him, *he* kills him instead."

My mind was racing a mile a minute as the rest of the story unfolded. Sebastian had unlocked a block that I had been fighting for weeks, and now that I knew the way around it, I felt confident I could finish the book on time.

"Thanks for your help," I said sincerely.

"Anytime. Shall we get back inside before the magic wears off and our asses freeze to this bench?"

"Yes, please. I need to dive in while everything is still fresh. Make some notes with plot points so I can make sure to hit them as I go."

We rushed back inside the house, slamming the door against the wind that had picked up again. I grabbed a bottle of water from the fridge and sat down, ready to get to work, when I remembered that Sebastian still had an issue with his book that he was stuck on.

"Hey, did you want to talk through your issue before I get started again?" I offered.

"Na, I'm good, but thanks."

"Are you sure? I don't mind helping. It's the least I can do after what you've done for me."

"Thanks, but this calls for research that I'm sure you don't want to be part of." He winked and grabbed his laptop from the table, taking it with him to the bed as I struggled to put two and two together.

"What kind of resear—"

My mouth snapped shut when I heard the sounds of moaning coming from his laptop before he plugged in his headphones and grinned. I turned around as quickly as possible and tried to ignore the fact that Sebastian was going to be sitting there watching porn for research.

Eight
Sebastian

You would think that being an erotic romance author would mean that not much could embarrass me or make me uncomfortable, but trying to watch porn with Brynlee in the room did just that. It wasn't that I was ashamed of what I was doing, but the flush on her cheeks when she realized it quickly brought out one on mine.

I had been stuck on a scene for a while and needed to find a fresh, new way for these people to fuck. That was the problem with the stuff I wrote. It felt boring and repetitive to me, while my fans were constantly expecting something over the top that pushed the limits. This series followed the same girl as she found her sexual freedom and had gone from one partner to multiple. It wasn't as simple as writing about her being spit-roasted but figuring out how to accurately describe three overly endowed cocks sliding into one hole.

I was a visual person, which meant that watching porn gave me the details I needed to easily get it down on paper. I hadn't spent long watching, but I could tell that Brynlee was more than curious every time she glanced my way over her shoulder. I wanted to tell her that she wasn't missing anything and that I was far more interested in what was happening in her book. Sure, I made a lot from my books because of how spicy they were, but I was growing tired of the constant sex and spending hours watching porn to get the scenes right.

My day hadn't been as productive as I would have liked, but when she got up and put her computer away at six, I followed suit. If she was calling it a day, I would too.

"I was going to bake some chicken for dinner tonight. Does that sound good?" I asked, joining her in the kitchen as she opened a can of Diet Coke and lifted it to her lips.

"You don't have to keep cooking for me."

"I'm making food for me anyway, Brynlee. There's not much difference with cooking one chicken breast versus two."

"I didn't expect to have power up here," she said with a heavy sigh, leaning against the counter. "I guess I should have planned better."

"It's not a problem at all. We have plenty of food, and I'm happy to cook."

"Can I help with anything?"

"Sure." I smiled at her as I opened the fridge and started pulling out the stuff for dinner.

I worked on breading the chicken to bake while Brynlee peeled potatoes to boil. We worked well in the small space we were given, moving around without getting in each other's way.

"Would you like some wine with dinner?" I asked once the chicken was in the oven.

"Yes, please."

I grabbed the bottle of wine while she reached into the cabinet for glasses. I was surprised that the cabin had everything we needed, given how small it was.

"I was thinking about getting some of the decorations out of the shed tomorrow and decorating in here," I said as I poured her a glass of white wine. "Would you be interested in helping?"

She lifted her eyebrows as she thought about it. I knew she had a deadline to meet with her manuscript, and I didn't want to deter her, but I couldn't help but think about how much fun it might be to do it together.

"You want to put up decorations together?" she asked softly, her head tilted slightly.

"Yeah… Is that okay?"

She shrugged and took a sip of wine as a small smile crept onto her face.

"I've never decorated with anyone before."

"What?" I pinched my brows together. "Not even with family growing up?"

She shook her head, and I couldn't help but notice the sadness that flashed through her eyes.

"I didn't have a family." She rubbed her lips together to keep the bottom one from quivering. "I was put into foster care when I was four. I don't remember anything before that, and we didn't do much for the holidays in the homes I went through. I never got adopted, and by the time I was out on my own, I didn't bother to decorate."

I had lifted my glass to take a drink and stopped.

"So you've *never* decorated for Christmas before?"

She shook her head again, lifting her glass and taking a sip.

"Is it something you might *want* to do?" I asked cautiously, not wanting to push her.

"I don't know. I guess it could be fun. I've never given it much thought. Growing up, I hated that I didn't have a family to do that stuff with, but I was with other kids who didn't have anyone, either. It was like we were special in a way, none of us missing out on anything more than the others. When I aged out of the system, it felt weird to decorate when it was always just me, and I wasn't decorating for anyone else. I guess I didn't feel like there was a reason to."

"Okay. That decides it," I said with so much enthusiasm that it made her giggle.

"Decides what?" she asked, her voice lighter than a few minutes ago.

"We're decorating the cabin tomorrow. We'll make a full day of it and pull out all the stops. It's going to be the best Christmas decorating day in the history of Christmas decorating days."

"I don't think that's a real thing," she said, brows pinched together as she grinned.

"It's not, but we're going to make it a real thing. Just wait and see."

Nine
Brynlee

"Do you need help?" I called, unable to see Sebastian behind the stacks of boxes piled up in the shed. It was freezing outside, but he had insisted on getting started first thing this morning. With his enthusiasm so palpable, I found myself joining in, instead of fighting him on it.

We'd already taken a few boxes into the cabin that were marked Christmas decorations, but it felt like there were dozens more. Bert wasn't kidding about having plenty of stuff to put up, but I thought it might have been a little obsessive when we found five artificial trees in boxes. Aside from the different light options, I couldn't see why there was a need for so many. But then Sebastian stood them side by side with the image of each on the front of the box facing me and my heart jumped at how beautiful the pre-lit seven-foot spruce looked with the white flocking snow. I knew immediately that was the tree I wanted.

"I got it," he grunted as another box slid off the shelf behind him.

"Are you sure?" My voice was more panicked as I heard a string of curse words slip from his lips.

"Yeah," he replied, breathing heavily as he came out, holding a few boxes. "Thankfully it's freezing balls out here, so I didn't even feel it when that one hit me in the back of the head."

"Oh no!" I covered my mouth, trying not to laugh. It wasn't that I thought it was funny; it was just my natural reaction whenever someone got hurt. "Are you okay?"

He nodded and let me grab one of the boxes from his stack before we headed back to the safety of the cabin. I waited for him to enter before pushing the door closed with my foot, thankful that the fire had kept it nice and toasty inside. We set our boxes down and took off our coats before looking around at the piles scattered around the room.

"Where do we start?" I asked nervously, chewing my nail.

"Let's get the tree up, then we'll go from there."

"Sounds like a plan. Just tell me what you want me to do."

He gave me a warm smile and then got started pulling the pieces out of the box and arranging them on the floor. I sat down across from him and watched as he worked, his muscles gently flexing under his t-shirt.

"Alright, here's the base. We'll start by putting these longer branches in and work our way up."

"This doesn't look as pretty as it does on the box," I said with a laugh as I put the first few branches in.

"That's because they're not fluffed out yet. Once we get all of them in, we'll go back and separate all the smaller branches. Then it'll look full like it did on the box."

I lowered my head and hated how embarrassed I felt for not knowing that. But I never had the privilege of helping to put up a tree because the few houses I went to that had trees were already decorated when I got there.

We worked quietly, our bodies brushing against each other

as we put the last few pieces in. I watched as Sebastian started separating them and did the same, feeling the tightness in my chest spread as the happiness washed over me as the tree grew more beautiful.

Once we were done, Sebastian cleared an area in the corner of the room by the windows and plugged it in. I held my breath, waiting for the lights to come on, but they didn't.

Sebastian stepped back, arms folded as he rubbed his thumb over the stubble on his jawline as he studied it.

"Is it broken?" I asked, trying to keep the disappointment out of my voice.

"It's likely just a bulb that is out and causing the whole strand to go out."

"How do you know which one it is?"

"I don't," he said lightly with a laugh. "I could try to figure it out, but I don't see any extra bulbs in the box. Honestly, it would be easier to wrap a new strand of lights than to figure out which one is out."

"Do you want me to go see if there are any strands of lights in the shed?" I offered.

"Na, I have a better idea."

He winked and gave me a grin that should have been a warning.

*****

"Are you sure this is safe?" I asked, gripping the handle above my head as Sebastian slowly drove down the mountain still covered in thick snow.

"I promise it is. I have it in four-wheel drive, which will give us more traction. Trust me, this is what trucks are made for."

"Okay." I gritted my teeth, my ass clenching tighter as we hit a bump.

I closed my eyes and kept my death grip on the handle as Sebastian maneuvered the rest of the way down the mountain.

"Alright, we're down," he said softly, placing a hand on my knee to get my attention.

I exhaled heavily as I opened my eyes and looked around.

"Thank goodness," I laughed.

"I told you we'd be just fine."

"Yeah, but the number of times you cussed on our way down didn't sound too reassuring," I joked.

"My ass is still clenched," he said, smiling at me.

"Mine too." I wasn't kidding. I was going to have to look at taking a long, hot bath tonight to get rid of the pain from it. I was already sore from sitting so long in the uncomfortable kitchen chairs.

"How about some coffee, and then we can do some shopping?" he offered, glancing in my direction as we stopped at a red light.

"Sure. That would be great."

I didn't want to tell him how thankful I was to be out of the cabin for a little while. Being there with him wasn't bad, but I hadn't gotten used to the limited space and lack of privacy. It reminded me too much of being in foster care, and I hated that feeling.

The light turned green, and he turned into a shopping center that looked promising, with plenty of shops lined up next to each other. We got out of the truck and stretched our legs before heading into Sugarplum Lattes.

There was a line to the door, but the heavenly aroma promised the wait would be worth it. I scanned the menu, not sure what I wanted, while Sebastian did the same.

"Do you know what you want?" he asked as we moved forward, the line clearing quickly as we approached the register.

"I don't know," I said with a sigh, still unsure, as the man at the counter smiled at us. "Everything looks too good to decide."

"Our peppermint mocha is always popular, but if you're looking for something less minty, I recommend either the gingerbread latte or the salted caramel espresso."

"What's your favorite?" I asked, reading the name *Sam* on his nametag.

"I usually go for the gingerbread latte," he replied, smiling. "It was one of my grandma's favorites and brings back happy memories this time of year."

"I'll do the gingerbread latte," I answered, feeling lighter already.

"Great choice," he said, looking from me to Sebastian. "What can I get for you?"

"I'll take the salted caramel espresso, please."

Sam punched the orders in and then took Sebastian's card, both of them refusing to acknowledge mine when I pulled it out and tried to pay for our drinks. Sebastian had given me a wink, which hadn't gone unnoticed by Sam based on the huge grin on his face.

I stepped to the side, people watching as Christmas music softly played through the speakers above us. It felt like I was in one of those Hallmark movies where the lost girl ends up in a quaint small town and falls in love with everything about it. It still felt weird that I was there with my favorite author, but it was kind of nice being the only one there who knew who he was.

Sebastian grabbed our drinks and led me out of the coffee shop with one hand on my lower back, guiding me out of the way of the people coming in. The cold air hit my face as soon as we stepped outside, but it was far less frigid than it was at the cabin.

We walked slowly, staying to the side so people could pass us if they wanted to, but surprisingly, no one was in a hurry. It was like everyone had all the time in the world, and no one was bothered by the snow and ice that covered the ground. Each shop was small and unique, making me want to stop in all of them. I didn't have anyone to buy Christmas gifts for, but that didn't stop me from wanting to pretend that I did. What would it feel like to have a family? To be excited as you find the perfect gift for them?

I had Macy, and she was the closest thing to family that I had. We had already given each other our gifts before I left, with the promise that we would FaceTime on Christmas day when we opened them. That didn't mean I couldn't get her another gift or two if I found the perfect one.

Sebastian held the door open to Sugarplum Gifts as I stepped inside, immediately warmed by the heater blasting through the small space. Christmas music floated through the air as an older woman wearing a sweater with bells on it approached us.

"Hi, welcome to Sugarplum Gifts. I'm Angie if you guys need anything."

"Thank you," I said with a warm smile, still impressed with how friendly everyone was.

We walked the aisles together, looking at different things that caught our eye. He was checking out a glass vase when I spotted an angel tree topper that brought tears to my eyes. I brushed my fingers across the thin fabric of her dress, entranced by the delicate figurine.

"She's beautiful," Sebastian said softly, his hand on my lower back again as he leaned in to talk.

"I don't know why, but I feel like I've seen this before. The second I saw it, it brought tears to my eyes," I whispered, fighting the emotions struggling to come out.

"Well then, that's a sign."

"What is?" I asked, turning slowly to face him as he reached in front of me to grab her.

"That she's meant to go home with you."

Before I could say anything or object, Sebastian cradled her in his arms as he made his way to the register. As we waited in line, I caught a glimpse of the price tag on the bottom and gasped.

"Sebastian, no," I whispered, tugging his arm to get his attention. "We have to put her back."

"Why? I thought you loved her?"

"I do, but I can't afford that. It's too much."

He gave me a devilish wink and then stepped up to the register. I inhaled sharply, unprepared for how to break it to the woman at the counter that we wouldn't be buying the tree topper. Thankfully, it wasn't the same woman who had greeted us because I couldn't stand the thought of breaking her heart this close to Christmas, given how fragile she looked.

"Hi, did you guys find everything alright?" She looked between us, waiting for an answer while the words stuck in my throat.

"Yes, thank you," Sebastian replied.

"Such a beautiful topper," she said with a wistful smile as she took it from him. "It reminds me of my aunt. More so, my cousin. It was her favorite, and she could always be found sitting in front of the tree, staring up at it."

Something in my chest tightened as she quickly blinked tears away. There was something about it that felt so familiar, but I couldn't put my finger on what it was or why.

"Does she still do that?" Sebastian asked, handing her his credit card.

"I'm sorry, what?" She shook her head and looked at him, confusion etched on her face.

"Your cousin. Does she still sit and stare at it?"

She took a deep breath and let it out slowly. Her fingers trembled as she wrapped it in paper to protect it.

"I don't know. That was over twenty years ago. My aunt died in a car accident, and I never saw my cousin again after that."

Ten
Sebastian

Brynlee was quiet after we left Sugarplum Gifts, and I couldn't tell whether it was because she was upset about me spending $200 on a tree topper or if something else was bothering her. We stopped in a few more shops and I was almost ready to suggest we go over to Sugar Faced Bar and have a drink or two to take the edge off.

I didn't know her well enough to pry or force her to open up to me if she didn't want to, even if I desperately wanted her to.

We finished shopping and then headed to Waldon's to grab some more groceries and the lights for the tree. I wanted to make Christmas as special for her as possible, even if we wouldn't be stuck together much longer. I would be lying if I said I wasn't disappointed when I saw how much snow had been cleared from the streets in town because I knew that meant there would be a good chance they would get to the roads leading in and out of town. Once that happened, we wouldn't have an excuse to stay holed up in the cabin together anymore.

"Anything special you feel like for dinner this week?" I asked as we headed to the meat department.

"Do you think we'll be stuck that long?"

I noticed the worry on her face but tried to convince myself that it wasn't because she *didn't* want to be there with me any longer.

"I don't know. I haven't heard anything about how clear the roads are outside of town yet. But just in case, we should get some groceries while we're here. I would hate to risk not getting enough and being unable to come back down if needed."

She nodded as she thought about it, her hands clasped firmly in front of her while I pushed the cart.

"Do you like meatloaf?" she asked, her green eyes sparkling at me.

"It's one of my favorites."

"Okay, we can do that tomorrow night if that works for you?"

"It does."

We kept walking as she added stuff to the cart, her teeth nervously chewing her bottom lip. Soon, we had a whole week's worth of fresh groceries, plus a handful of frozen pizzas because you could never have too much pizza.

As we got to the register, I lined myself up so Brynlee couldn't get past me as I unloaded the cart.

"Did you find everything you needed?" the woman asked as she started ringing us up.

"Yes, thank you."

She looked down the conveyor belt at the items we were getting and then back to me with worry in her eyes.

"Are you sure that will be enough?"

My brow furrowed as I tried to figure out what she was referring to.

"Enough for what?"

"To get you two through the storm," she said urgently, swiping items over the scanner and passing them down the other side to be bagged. "It's going to be even bigger than the last one, and they expect it to shut everything in town down for at least a few days, maybe a week. I just hope it doesn't ruin Frosty Fest. That would be a shame if it didn't happen this year."

"Another storm?" Brynlee added, leaning in to hear the conversation better.

"Yeah, it's going to be a real doozy. Everyone is stocking up on the essentials. Do you guys have plenty of bottled water and batteries at home?"

"We weren't aware another storm was coming," I answered, clearing my throat. "I'll pay for this, and then go grab a few more things." My answer was more for Brynlee but seemed to appease the cashier as she nodded, clearly relieved by my decision. We had plenty of groceries to get us through the week, but now that I knew a bigger storm was moving in, I wanted to make sure we would be covered for several weeks in case I couldn't safely make it back to town.

"Have they cleared the roads out of town yet?" Brynlee asked eagerly.

"Oh, no, dear. They haven't had a chance to. Today was our first good day since the last storm hit. Everyone finally made it out of their houses, but it was to grab supplies and maybe get some shopping done. Typically we all wait for Frosty Fest to get our gifts for everyone, but if it doesn't happen this year, most of us will be screwed." She had been talking aloud but didn't realize we were still there. "Sorry, excuse my language," she apologized, her cheeks red with embarrassment. "We're all just a little flustered with the biggest blizzard Sugarplum Falls has ever seen."

Brynlee sank back beside me, her shoulders slumped.

"We can run this stuff out to the truck real quick, then I'll come back and grab what we need for the storm," I offered.

"No, I'll come help you. It'll be faster with two of us."

"You don't have to take it to your truck," the cashier said, ringing up the final items. "Just park it over there until you're ready."

"But what if someone steals it?" I asked, immediately realizing that stuff like that must not happen here by the look of shock on her face.

"No one would do such a thing. You two go finish your shopping, and I'll be here when you're done."

She handed me the receipt and then pushed our cart against the wall across from her. I took a deep breath and tried not to look too excited to be stuck in a cabin with Brynlee for a little while longer.

Eleven
Brynlee

By the time we got back to the cabin and unloaded the truck, the snow was coming down in sheets while the wind made it nearly impossible to breathe. I unpacked the groceries and put the perishable stuff away while Sebastian gathered more firewood and brought it in. He said we should have enough to last a week or two, but he'd also taken the time to haul a few large pieces of wood into the garage so they could dry before we needed them.

I decided to take the initiative to get dinner started while he arranged the wood by the fireplace. I needed to clear my head, but that would have to wait until after we ate, when I would hopefully be able to escape for a bit in a long, hot bath. For now, I would distract myself with cooking and pray it was edible.

"Dinner smells good," Sebastian said, joining me in the kitchen as he washed his hands.

"Thank you. The weather made me crave something warm and hearty, so I'm making beef stew. It should be ready soon."

"Anything I can help with?" He leaned against the counter and casually crossed his ankles, the cream color of his sweater making the brown in his eyes pop.

"You can get the rolls ready if you want?"

"Will do." He pushed off and grabbed the bag of premade rolls from the counter. "This is basically a sin, though."

"What is?" I tilted my head to see him as I stirred the contents of the pot, the aroma making my mouth water.

"That we're eating store-bought bread. A stew that smells that good deserves freshly baked bread."

"I agree," I said with a laugh, setting the spoon down. "But unfortunately, that is not a skill set that I have, so we're stuck with those."

"Well, tomorrow I'll make us some bread. It looks like there's plenty of stew for leftovers."

I scrunched my nose and looked at the stock pot full I had made.

"I grew up cooking for a lot of people because there were always a lot of us in each home. I haven't quite mastered the art of making smaller portions," I admitted.

"Do you cook a lot for yourself?"

"Sometimes. But I tend to rely on delivery and frozen pizza."

He lowered his head and shook it.

"Brynlee, Brynlee, Brynlee," he tsked. "You can't live off that stuff. It's not good for you."

I shrugged and allowed my lips to curl up into a smile.

"It's not like I have anyone else to cook for. It takes too much time, and I usually have a deadline I'm up against. It's quick and easy to just put in an order and write until it comes. Little clean up. Everyone is happy."

"I knew it," he said happily, giving me the biggest grin I'd ever seen.

"Knew what? That I don't like cooking?"

"Nope. That it was fate."

"What was?"

"You. Me. The blizzard. Getting stranded together in this cabin. Fate brought us together so I could help show you the way."

"And what way is that exactly?"

"The way to happiness."

"I hate to burst your bubble, but I am happy." I felt the lie burn my tongue as I said it. I wasn't sure I even knew what happiness was, given that my life hadn't been filled with much of it.

"Of course you are, but there's no such thing as *too happy*. So it's now my goal in life, my mission, if you will, to make you happier. Project Make Brynlee Happy is now commencing!"

I shook my head and laughed, giving the stew one final stir.

"Well, then, I guess we shall start this new project by celebrating that the stew is done, and I managed to make it without burning anything."

"A perfect cause for celebration."

Sebastian grabbed the bowls and held them steady while I served us. We sat at the small table, warmed by the fire, as a red candle burned in between us. It felt almost romantic.

I knew that it was just dinner with two people who had been thrown together during a freak blizzard, nothing more. Even if my heart pitter-pattered at the possibility…

Twelve
Sebastian

The cabin was quiet—too quiet—as Brynlee soaked in the tub, and I sat on the bed, flipping through the channels on the TV, looking for something to watch. She had grabbed some stuff at Waldon's earlier, and the sweet scent floating under the bathroom door was pleasantly relaxing. I couldn't tell exactly what it was, but it reminded me of the lavender lotion my mom always used when I was younger.

I knew I should have been writing instead of watching TV, but it was late, and my brain was fried. I had plotted the next few chapters, but I just wasn't feeling the story, which made it that much harder to write. I was genuinely enjoying spending time with Brynlee, and that made me want to write even less. We hadn't finished decorating the cabin yet, but I was hoping to carve some time out of the day tomorrow for that.

A rerun of an old cop show played on the TV, but my mind was still focused on Brynlee and her reaction to the tree topper I'd bought her. Her eyes had so much emotion that they pulled me in, and I knew I had to get it for her.

Feeling restless, I got up and paced the small space of the cabin, looking for something to do. The rest of the bags from earlier were piled up in the corner of the kitchen, out of the way, as we had only focused on putting the perishable stuff away.

I grabbed them and lined them up on the counter, putting the canned goods in the cabinets and replenishing the bottles of water in the pantry. We'd also bought a few extra packs of toilet paper, just in case, but there wasn't any room to store them, so I left them in the corner. Once things were put away, I grabbed the strand of lights from the counter and got to work wrapping it around the tree.

I debated waiting for Brynlee so she could help me, but since it was more of a one-person job, I went ahead and did it. I couldn't wait to see her face when she came out and found the tree lit up since she was so disappointed earlier when it didn't turn on.

We would get the ornaments put on the tree tomorrow, including the few we'd picked out together today. But for now, it already felt a lot more like Christmas, with the beautiful tree lit up in the corner of the room. I couldn't wait to see it tomorrow with the snowy landscape behind it through the windows.

I sat on the bed and watched *It's A Wonderful Life* while Brynlee finished her bath. It was one of my favorite holiday movies, but I found myself wishing I was watching it with Brynlee instead. It was odd how I was growing fond of her so quickly and how much I loved the excitement of *wanting* to spend time with someone. It had been a long time since I'd felt it.

The movie was almost over when the bathroom door opened and Brynlee emerged wearing a pair of plaid thermal pajamas and her hair wrapped in a towel. She started taking it down but stopped when she spotted the tree.

Her eyes lit up, and her hands flew to her mouth as a smile exploded on her lips.

"It's BEAUTIFUL!" she squealed, coming around the corner to see it better. "Oh my gosh, Sebastian, it's amazing!"

I got up and stood beside her, admiring the tree.

"I'm glad you like it."

"Like it?" she turned and looked up at me. "I love it. It's the most beautiful Christmas tree I've ever seen."

My heart swelled in my chest as I fought the urge to reach over and pull her to me. She wasn't mine to hold, but that didn't mean I couldn't enjoy these special moments with her.

74

Thirteen
Brynlee

The lights sparkled on the tree, but my favorite were the white ones. They looked like snowflakes that had fallen and landed perfectly on the tips of the green branches. Someone bounced me on their knee, holding tightly so they didn't drop me.

"Be careful with her, Had," a stern voice warned.

"I will," a child answered.

I looked around, trying to see who was holding me, but everything was blurry. There were sounds of adults talking in the distance, but I couldn't hear what they were saying. Loud whispers turned into angry sounds, and I started to cry. Arms wrapped tighter around me as we bounced faster, but it didn't make the loud noises less scary.

I cried louder, and someone picked me up. It wasn't the little hands holding me anymore. These ones were stronger. Sturdier.

"Shhh, it's okay," she whispered, holding me to her chest. "Do you see the angel? Isn't she beautiful? Just like my sweet Ma—"

The sound of a tree branch whipping the window startled me as I jumped up in bed, sweat pouring down my back. My chest heaved as I struggled to catch my breath, desperately looking around to see where I was. The dream had felt so real, the voice so familiar.

"Hey, what's wrong?" Sebastian asked, sitting up beside me and turning on the lamp.

I shook my head, my throat tight and burning as I tried to blink away the tears that prickled my eyes.

"I don't know," I stammered. "A bad dream, I guess?"

I rubbed my eyes, upset with myself for being so emotional over something that hadn't happened.

"This is so stupid." I grabbed a tissue from the end table and blotted my eyes before blowing my nose. "I don't even know why I'm so upset. It was just a dream, but it felt so real. It was like I was bac…"

I paused as the words stuck in my throat, unable to speak them.

"It was like what?" he asked softly, shifting on the bed as he turned to look at me.

"It was like I was at a house that I remembered. Somewhere I had been to before." I looked past him and spotted the angel tree topper we had put on before bed. "I was little, and someone was holding me while I looked at the tree. There was a topper just like that one." I pointed to it as the tears fell down my cheeks.

"I'm sorry, Brynlee. I didn't mean to upset you with it."

"You didn't," I assured him. "It was just a stupid dream. That's all."

"But was it?" He tilted his head and studied me.

"Yeah. Of course. What else would it be?"

He worked his jaw back and forth before answering me.

"What if it wasn't just a dream? What if it was a memory instead?"

I turned to face him, pulling the pillow against my chest as a barrier.

"What do you mean?"

He took a deep breath and locked eyes with me.

"I'm not trying to upset you, but what if it wasn't a dream and was a memory instead? You mentioned earlier that you felt like you had seen it before, that it brought tears to your eyes."

"So?"

"So what if it was a memory from your childhood? Sometimes, those strong emotional reactions can pull up memories that we've buried deep inside. Maybe it wasn't a dream, but rather your subconscious giving you confirmation that you had seen it before."

"I already told you, I don't remember much from before I went into the system. And I can guarantee you we didn't have that tree topper in any of the homes I went to."

"What if it was from *before* then? A memory with your parents?"

A chill snaked up my spine, forcing me to grab the blankets and pull them tighter around me. My nose burned as the threat of more tears loomed in the distance.

"I highly doubt that it is," I said, my voice cracking as I wiped the tears from my cheeks. I didn't want to entertain the thought and be disappointed when it turned out to be just a dream and nothing more.

"But what if it was?" he pushed. "I know you're going to think I'm crazy, but what if it was all fate, Brynlee?"

I stared at him with furrowed brows, waiting for him to continue. He pulled his shoulders back and smiled softly at me.

"What is the likelihood that you and I would be crossing paths at the same time and get stranded together in Sugarplum Falls?"

"I don't know," I said with a shrug. "I guess pretty good, given that we were both passing through when the storm hit."

"Yeah, but think about it—we both ended up at the *same* hotel at the *same* time. You could have easily gone to the other hotel. I could have been late because I stopped for gas. But none of that happened. We were destined to be at that hotel at the same time."

"Okay, but what does that have to do with the dream?"

"Everything, Brynlee. You got stranded in Sugarplum Falls for a reason. We randomly decided to go into town yesterday, which, according to the locals, was the first decent day they've had since the first storm hit. But something told us to go. We took the time to go shopping and ended up in a store that had a tree topper that reminded you of something you couldn't put your finger on. Then you have a dream about that same tree topper, and it takes you back to your childhood."

"Yeah, but none of that matters if I can't even remember my childhood, Sebastian. I hate to break it to you, but those days are long past me. I don't have a family. I don't have anyone who knew me before I went into foster care, and I sure as hell didn't have anyone who cared about me after.

Even *if* it were a memory from my childhood, I don't have anyone who can confirm or deny it."

"I know." He sighed heavily. "I'm just saying that maybe this is fate's way of giving you closure on that part of your life. What if all of these things are happening for a reason?"

"I have all the closure I need." I took a deep breath and held it before slowly letting it out. "I don't know much about my childhood other than my parents walked away from me and never looked back."

Fourteen
Sebastian

The next few days had been quieter than expected with Brynlee shutting down after her dream the other night. I didn't want to push her to talk about it, so I gave her as much time and space as possible while she worked through whatever she needed. We didn't get around to decorating like I wanted to, but at least we were both being productive with our writing.

It was less than a week until Christmas, and the worst of the storm had finally passed. We lost power for a bit, but thankfully, the backup generator worked beautifully, so we hadn't even noticed. It would still be a few days before I could safely get down the mountain to go into town, but I wasn't worried about it since we had stocked up on food and basic necessities.

I was heading into seven hours straight of writing, only taking a small break here and there to stretch and snack when needed. I'd made good progress on my manuscript and had officially reached the halfway point, but my brain was fried. I saved what I had, then shut down my computer and put it away.

Brynlee was in the kitchen, looking through the fridge, when I joined her. It was after seven, and neither of us had stopped to have a real meal yet, which was evident by my stomach's loud growl.

She looked over her shoulder, staring wide-eyed as her leggings stretched tight across her ass. I looked away, feeling bad for checking her out.

"I was just looking for something to make for dinner," she said, standing up and closing the door.

"Find anything good?" I asked, clearing my throat as I tried to ignore the subtle bulge in my pants from staring so hard at her ass.

"I'm kinda tired, so I thought a frozen pizza would be quick and easy. You?"

"I could get down with some pizza if you're willing to share."

"I'll share the pizza, but only if you share the chocolate truffles you got from Sugarplum Sweets," she said, smiling coyly.

"Fine. I'll share my truffles, but you have to share your port wine."

"Deal."

She extended her hand to shake mine, but instead of thinking rationally about it, I grabbed it and pulled her into me. She stumbled slightly as her body fell against mine, her hands splaying across my chest as my arms wrapped around her lower back.

"I have one more condition," I said, my voice low in her ear.

"Okay," she breathed, looking at me under thick, dark lashes. "What's that?"

"We eat in bed and watch a Christmas movie."

She looked back and forth as if thinking about it, but I could see the humor in her eyes. I dug my fingers into her sides, tickling her until she giggled and squirmed against me.

"Okay, okay," she laughed. "It's a deal. But I get to pick the movie."

I wrapped my arms around her again, not sure why it didn't feel weird. But neither of us seemed to mind, so I wasn't willing to rush the moment.

"No deal. You're not picking the movie."

"Why not?" She tilted her head and pouted at me.

"Because you're going to make us watch some horror movie or a true crime documentary."

"So? What's wrong with that?" She batted her eyes playfully.

"Those aren't Christmassy!"

"They are to me. Nothing says happy holidays like a bone-chilling murder to solve."

"Something's wrong with you," I teased, shaking my head.

"Fine, you big baby. You can pick the movie."

"Fine."

"But I'm picking the pizza," she insisted, jutting her chin out as she pulled away. "Hope you like pineapple."

I lowered my head in defeat. She knew how much I hated

pineapple on pizza after we talked about topping choices at the store. We had grabbed a handful of options, so neither of us was stuck with one we didn't like.

By the time the food was ready, I had set the bed up for us with blankets and pillows galore. I wanted to make it a fun movie night, but I also couldn't help but feel like it was a date. I knew it wasn't, but something had shifted between us when I pulled her into me earlier, and I desperately wanted to explore whatever it was.

"Pizza is ready," she called from the kitchen while I scrolled through the movie options on TV. Bert had several streaming services, giving us a broad selection to choose from, which was nice.

"I'll be right there. Just picking a movie."

"You better pick a good one. None of that *Love Actually* crap," she teased over her shoulder.

"You know what? Just for that, that's what we're going to watch."

I selected the movie but didn't press play, so it wouldn't start before we were ready. She was standing at the counter with her hands on her hips as she playfully glared at me.

"I went out of my way to make you a nice dinner, and you repay me by picking that movie?"

"You made pizza with pineapple, knowing that I hate it," I objected, invading her space as I stepped closer to her.

"Are you sure about that?"

Her eyes trailed behind me and I looked back to see two pizzas on the counter, one special and one Hawaiian.

"You made me a different pizza?"

She nodded.

"Thank you. That was very nice of you."

"Does that mean you'll pick something else to watch?"

"Nope. Not a chance." I handed her a plate and stepped to the side to let her go first.

Fifteen
Brynlee

The movie wasn't bad, but it definitely wasn't as good as the chocolate truffles we devoured in one sitting.

"So, what did you think?" Sebastian asked, turning to face me on the bed.

"It was okay." I shrugged, scrunching my nose as his eyebrows shot up on his forehead.

"Just *okay*?"

"It was kind of slow and predictable."

"But didn't it make you feel all warm and fuzzy inside?"

"No, I'm sorry," I apologized with a laugh. "But the truffles did."

He shook his head and shoved a hand through his short hair before falling against his pillows.

"It wasn't a *terrible* movie," I added, feeling bad that I hadn't loved it.

"But?"

"But I've seen better."

"You've seen a better Christmas movie?" he questioned, giving me an incredulous look.

"I have."

"Okay, I'll play along. What was it?"

I chewed my lower lip as he watched.

"Never mind. I don't want to tell you."

"Nope. You have to. Spill it."

I shook my head, still chewing my lip.

"Brynlee," he warned, leaning closer.

"I'm not going to tell you because you're just going to make fun of me and tell me it's not a good Christmas movie."

"Try me."

I took a deep breath and let it out heavily, playing up how hard this was for me.

"Fine." I stuck my tongue out at him. "It's *The Nightmare Before Christmas*."

He closed his eyes as if pained to hear it, rubbing a hand against his forehead.

"That's not a Christmas movie," he objected.

"Sure it is!"

"No, it's not. It's about a guy who gets jealous of the attention Christmas Town gets and schemes to take over the holiday. It's not even a Christmas movie—it's a Halloween one."

"Well, let's agree to disagree. Either way, it warms my heart," I teased, even though I hadn't seen the movie—I wasn't going to tell him that, though.

"It's five days until Christmas, and you think an anti-Christmas movie is the best Christmas movie there is," he said, letting his head fall into his hands. "We have so much work to do in such a little time, Brynlee."

I laughed softly, shifting on the bed to get comfortable again.

"Can I ask you something?" I asked, turning so I could face him.

"Is it what the best Christmas movie is?" he teased, lowering his hands so I could see his face again.

"No," I laughed. "I think we're going to have to agree to disagree on that one. This is a personal question."

"Go for it."

"We've been cooped up in this cabin together for seven days, and I haven't seen you call anyone since we've been here. Not that it's an issue or anything, I guess I was just wondering if you had family you were heading home to for Christmas or if you were spending it by yourself, like me?"

"Nope. I wasn't heading anywhere in particular this year. I guess, in a way, I just got on the road and hoped I would find myself along the way."

"Do you usually spend the holidays alone?" I asked softly. It had been on my mind for a few days now, but I hadn't been able to figure out how to ask him what his deal was without sounding rude.

"I used to go home for the holidays, but my relationship with my parents has grown apart over the years, so I stopped going a while back."

"Oh. I'm sorry." I shook my head, feeling embarrassed for asking.

"Don't be. We haven't had a good relationship in years. I don't miss being around my belligerent drunk father or watching my mom pop pills to numb herself to it. I realized that Christmas used to be fun when I was little, but now that I'm 32, I don't have the patience for their bullshit."

"Some of my foster parents were the same way. They were more concerned with where the money came from than with caring for the kids they had in their home. I always hated when I got put with the mean ones."

"I'm sorry you had such a hard childhood, Brynlee. No one deserves that."

"I'm sorry I turned this into such a depressing conversation." I tried to laugh and make light of it, but Sebastian stayed serious.

"Should we find another movie and see if it puts us in the Christmas spirit?" I offered, reaching for the remote.

"No," he said, shaking his head. "I have something better in mind."

Sixteen
Sebastian

I pulled up my Christmas playlist on Spotify and turned it up while Brynlee and I worked on finishing decorating the cabin. The mood had shifted from the depressing conversation we had after the movie, and the smile on her face as she hung an ornament on the tree was priceless.

We had gone through the bags of stuff we'd purchased in town and decided to make the tree our own instead of using any of the decorations Bert had. I loved seeing how her eyes lit up every time we added another ornament, pure excitement and joy shining in them.

"Now, while we might remain undecided on what the best Christmas movie is, I think we can both agree that decorating is better than anything else we could have done tonight," I said, reaching above her head to hang an ornament.

Her cheeks flushed a cute shade of light pink as she ducked away from me and moved around to the back of the tree. I didn't want to embarrass her, so I let it go. But deep down, I was curious about what she had been thinking to get that kind of reaction.

"It is pretty fun," she agreed, barely peeking her head around the bushy tree to smile at me. "I'm glad we picked our own decorations. I like that better than using ones someone else picked."

"I agree."

We kept hanging the glass ball ornaments, moving around each other in the tiny space as music floated around us.

"How's it going with your manuscript?" I asked, knowing that she was getting down to the wire with Christmas Eve being only four days away.

"It's getting there." She sighed heavily and came around to the front of the tree, smiling as she stared at it. "I have twenty thousand words left, more or less. I thought I was close to being done, but then a plot twist happened. Now I have to work that in, which threw my schedule off."

"Do you ever think about writing other genres?" I busied myself with putting more hooks through the last few ornaments, hoping she didn't read through the real reason I was asking.

"Not really. I occasionally read romance, but I don't entertain the thought of writing it."

"Why not? Romantic suspense would be a great transition for you since you've already nailed the suspense side with your thrillers."

"I don't think I would be very good at it." She made a face that pulled a chuckle from deep in my chest.

"Writing romance isn't that hard," I said, handing her an ornament to hang.

"It is if you don't know anything about it." She laughed, but I felt something tug at my heart, wondering if she had ever been in love.

"I make up more than half of what I write," I admitted.

"Trust me, it's easy enough. Just like you do a great job of writing thrillers, but I'm sure you don't pull from personal experience of stalking and murdering people."

She arched an eyebrow and gave me a sly smile.

"And all this time *you* were worried that *I* might kill you?"

Her laughter filled the space between us, and I found my fingers itching to reach over and touch her.

"I watch a lot of true crime shows," she explained. "It's not like I'm watching a bunch of porn and pulling inspiration from that."

As if realizing what she was implying, her cheeks turned scarlet, and her hand flew to her mouth.

"I'm sorry, I wasn't insinuating—"

"You're fine, Brynlee," I assured her, letting my hand pull hers down, even though I was still trying to keep them to myself. "I watch porn when needed for a scene, but that's not the romance part. That's just the physical act of them doing it and getting the details right. Writing romance is about so much more than that."

"Like what?"

"Like building tension. Creating a connection between your characters. Romance is about so much more than the physical act of sex."

"I wouldn't know the first step of how to write something like that," she replied softly, lowering her eyes. "I've never been with anyone who took the time for romance. The most I know about it is from reading it, and that doesn't teach me enough to be able to write it."

"Like I said, it can be the simplest of things that pull them together."

I stepped closer, lowering my mouth to her ear as I spoke softly.

"For example, him gently brushing his arm across her back as he reaches for something. It's an innocent touch, but the chemistry sizzling beneath the surface is ignited by it. Hearts start racing. Pupils dilate. Palms get clammy. Their bodies react to each other, speaking a language only they can hear."

I could feel the heat from her body as my hand rested on her lower back while the other reached to the table to grab the candy cane ornament.

"It's about trust. Communication. Knowing that each touch is wanted. Craved. Yearned for. And then building the tension between them. Making them work for the release they want. The climax they need."

"You make it sound so easy," she whispered, her body leaning into my touch.

"It is." I stepped in front of her, allowing my hand to trail around her waist and rest on her hip. My legs braced her, pinning her in as I walked her the few steps back until she was up against the wall.

Her eyes flashed with a mix of excitement and arousal, and I felt an immediate reaction in my groin.

"The build-up is so worth it if you do it right," I whispered, lifting her chin with my finger as my body rested against hers. Slowly, I moved my head, my lips feathering against hers before moving to the side of her face and hovering over the pulse point in her neck.

I could feel her body reacting beneath me. The heavy rise and fall of her chest. The way her legs parted to welcome me in.

"I could kiss you right now, Brynlee. Give your body every single thing she's asking for."

My fingers splayed across her skin, her shirt riding up slightly as she wrapped her arms around my neck. I wanted to inch up further and caress her pebbled nipples that were poking through the thin fabric.

"Yes," she whimpered, pulling me into her as her mouth found mine.

I knew that I should pull back and stop this, but when she fisted her hands in the back of my shirt, I knew neither of us would be able to stop now.

Seventeen
Brynlee

"Don't stop," I panted, grabbing Sebastian's clothes as I tried to free him of them.

I didn't know what had come over me, but I knew I wouldn't regret whatever this was. My body was on fire for the first time, and I wasn't going to stop now. No one had ever touched me in such a way to elicit this kind of response, and I didn't want it to stop any time soon.

"Are you sure you want to do this, Brynlee?" he asked between kisses. "I wasn't trying to push you into anything. I was just trying to give an example of how to—"

"You're a very good teacher. A+. Now, let's complete this lesson and move to the extra credit, okay?"

He chuckled and lifted me to his hips, carrying me to the bed before dropping me on it.

I reached for my shirt to take it off, and he shook his head.

"I want the pleasure of undressing you."

I licked my lips and lowered my hands to my side, watching as he reached behind and pulled his shirt off. Thankfully, it was warm enough in the cabin that we didn't need to wear layers because I couldn't imagine letting him wear clothes ever again after seeing the perfectly sculpted body hiding beneath those sweaters he'd been wearing.

He stepped out of his jeans and tossed them to the side after retrieving a condom from his wallet. His black boxer briefs did nothing to hide the monster lurking inside—just like I predicted.

I was getting more impatient by the second, desperate for his touch or any contact that could quell the aching inside. My eyes locked with his as my hand dipped beneath the waistband of my leggings and slid into my panties.

He pulled his bottom lip between his teeth and watched, making no effort to rush to touch me.

"You can have a turn if you'd like," I offered a little too eagerly.

"I'm enjoying the show, but it would be better without the clothes. Mind if I help take them off now?"

"By all means, be my guest."

He climbed onto the bed, kissing my lips tenderly as his fingers pulled my pants down my legs. I moaned as he kissed my neck, my finger sliding between my lips.

"These too," he growled, waiting for me to lift my butt so he could take off my panties.

It felt a little weird to be on full display in front of him as I touched myself, but surprisingly, it didn't stop me from inching my way toward an orgasm.

"You're so fucking wet, Brynlee."

"You did this to me," I admitted, slipping another finger inside and arching my back. "I'm so ready to come already."

"Show me," he encouraged, his voice low and gravely. He stood up and lowered his briefs, allowing his cock to spring free. "Give me something to watch as I stroke my cock for you."

I focused on his hand, licking my lips as I watched the way his fingers wrapped tightly around and gripped it.

"You want it in your mouth, don't you?"

His dirty words were sending me over the edge, yet I couldn't get enough. I nodded and grinned when he walked over and stood in front of me. I pulled my fingers out, coating him with my wetness, loving how his eyes darkened.

I stroked him a few times, the weight in my hand making my pussy ache with need. My eyes locked with his as I leaned forward and took him in my mouth before fingering myself again.

His head fell back for a brief second as he hit the back of my throat, then he grabbed a fistful of my hair and held my head in place as I sucked harder. I slid two fingers inside my pussy, fucking myself fast and hard, the sound loud enough to be heard over the roar of the fire, but I didn't care. I could feel him harden more in my mouth and knew he was as aroused by it as I was.

I brought my free hand up and wrapped it around his cock, jacking off the portion that didn't fit in my mouth. I wanted to give him the best blow job I could while also getting myself off. I did the combo move I had mastered, twisting my hand in circles as my lips slid up and down his shaft before hollowing out my cheeks and sucking.

He hissed through his teeth, gripping my head harder as I rubbed my clit.

"Fuck, Brynlee," he growled. "You're going to make me come just watching you touch yourself. That fucking beautiful pussy glistening for me. If you don't want me to come down your throat, you better stop sucking me off."

I shook my head the best I could, given his grip on it, then spread my legs wider, watching as his eyes locked on my fingers as they rubbed my clit harder.

Within seconds, I felt the spasms as the first wave of pleasure rolled through me. I closed my eyes and kept rubbing, allowing the pleasure to keep taking over as he shot ropes of hot, salty cum down the back of my throat.

Eighteen
Sebastian

"So, what were you saying about building tension?" Brynlee teased, cuddled into my side as we laid on the bed, both of us coming down from our climaxes.

"I think we've mastered the sexual tension part," I said with a laugh, softly tickling her side. "But we haven't even covered the non-sexual stuff yet."

"I guess I was just eager to get the lesson started."

"You're quite the student, though I'll admit you taught me a thing or two."

"Oh yeah? Like what?"

"That it was possible to come with my cock down your throat while you fingered yourself and got off. I swear, Brynlee, that was hotter than anything I've seen before."

"Even with porn?"

"Especially with porn. I hardly ever watch it to get off. It's usually just for research purposes, and when I'm in that mindset, the last thing I'm thinking about is getting myself off."

"I guess I could see that. I watch true crime shows to help with my writing, but I don't feel a strong urge to go out and kill someone."

I pulled my head back and looked down at her.

"Yeah, that's not really the same thing. But okay."

She elbowed me in the ribs, making me laugh.

"I'm just teasing. But I'm also pretty relieved you haven't had to do any *research* while we've been here. You know, just in case something changed and you decided now was the time to act on those intrusive thoughts."

"Don't worry. I think we're both safe from worrying that either of us is out to kill the other," she assured me with a laugh.

"I wouldn't be so certain. I'm still out to get you," I said, my voice low in her ear.

She looked up and arched a brow at me.

"Oh yeah?"

"Yup. I only got to *watch* earlier. Now I'm ready to explore your body with my hands and tongue."

A soft gasp escaped her plump lips before I leaned down and captured her mouth.

I slid down beside her, lying next to her as my tongue took its time caressing her lips before moving down her neck. My fingers eagerly trailed down her skin, feeling the goosebumps that spread across it with each touch.

She arched her back as I kissed her collarbone, desperate for more. I grabbed the bottom of her shirt and pulled it off before working the clasp on her bra so I could finally suck her puckered nipples. My mouth was hot against her skin, the temperature in the cabin dropping as the fire started to die out. I knew I needed to throw another log in there soon, but right now, I was too focused on touching her.

I climbed over her, sliding my hand up her thigh as my tongue teased her nipple before pulling it into my mouth. I loved the way she hissed in response before digging her nails into my back and scratching.

"Mmmm," she moaned, spreading her legs to allow my hand inside.

Her pussy was still wet for me when I slid a finger in, pumping for a few seconds before inserting another one. I released one nipple, then moved to the other, greedily sucking as she cried out and bucked her hips.

My cock hardened, ready to be inside her as I continued to rub her. The way she clenched around me made it hard not to blow my load right then and there as I imagined her doing that to my dick.

"You're so tight," I growled, letting her nipple pop free as my thumb worked her clit while she bit down on my shoulder. "I want to fuck you so bad."

"Do it. Fuck me. Now."

I reached over and grabbed the condom, tearing the wrapper with my teeth. I wanted to go all night with her, but I wasn't sure I would even last a few minutes—which was saying a lot about how fucking hard I was for her.

I quickly sheathed myself, then lined up at her entrance, slowly pushing inside as we stared into each other's eyes. It wasn't something I had done with a woman before, but it didn't feel wrong with Brynlee.

Once I was fully seated inside her, I held still for a moment to let her get used to my size. Then she started rolling her hips beneath me, encouraging me to give it to her.

"Fuck me hard, Sebastian," she begged, clawing my back again.

I lifted her legs to my shoulder and pinned them together with one arm as I sat on my knees, balls deep inside her. I slowly ground my hips against her, pushing inside as she moaned in pleasure. Then I pulled out and slammed inside her.

"Ah!" she cried out, closing her legs tighter. "Yes!"

I grinned as I pulled out again and slammed harder into her. The sound of my balls slapping against her ass each time I did it was pure music to my ears. I thrusted harder and harder until I couldn't take it anymore and let her legs fall to the bed.

"On your hands and knees," I commanded, pulling out of her so she could change position. I handed her a pillow to brace herself, then lined up at her entrance and slid inside again.

This time, I didn't pull out and slam into her like I had before. Instead, I gripped her hips, held her steady, and fucked her so hard and deep that both of us were crying out while I rubbed her clit and brought her to another orgasm.

Nineteen

Brynlee

It felt oddly comfortable to be cuddled against Sebastian after we had sex, both fully satisfied as we fought to stay awake. While I would normally argue that I wasn't the kind of girl who would jump into bed with a guy after seven days, it really didn't feel like it had been *only* seven days. It felt longer, given we were spending every hour of every day together.

"I saw on the news earlier that the roads in town should be clear by tomorrow morning," Sebastian said, rubbing his fingers up and down my arm as I curled into his chest. "I thought about heading into town and checking out the Frosty Fest they keep talking about."

"Yeah?" I tilted my head up to see him.

His hair was beautifully disheveled, and I loved the scruff that had grown with him not shaving since we got here. It gave him a rough, mountain man vibe I was into.

"Wanna go with me?"

"Sure. It sounds like fun, and I need to get out of the cabin for a bit."

"Cool. There's a parade in the morning we can go to if you'd like. If not, we can just do the shopping stuff in the mall, so we're not stuck in the cold."

"Sounds good," I replied through a yawn.

"You ready for bed?"

"Yeah. I don't think I could stay awake if I tried."

"Let's get some rest. We have a fun and busy day ahead of us."

I thought about rolling over to my side of the bed and giving him some space, but before I could overthink anything, he reached up and turned the light off before wrapping his arms around me. My body melted into his, and within seconds, my eyes fluttered closed as I drifted to sleep.

******

By the time we got to town the next day, we had already missed the parade. The road down the mountain was still covered in ice, and even though Sebastian had four-wheel drive, that hadn't stopped us from sliding along it in spots. My knuckles were white from gripping the handle so tightly, and my stomach was in a knot when we parked and went into the mall.

Thankfully, it was nice and warm inside, a welcome change from the below-freezing temperatures outside. We found a place with coffee and stopped there first, needing the warmth and caffeine fix before we started exploring Frosty Fest.

The space was beautifully decorated with warm lights strung across the ceiling and tall trees decorated with fake snow and delicate-looking glass ornaments. A giant stage sat in the middle of the room where Mr. and Mrs. Claus were set up to take pictures with kids, with vendor booths scattered around it so the parents could window shop while their children waited their turn.

We sipped our lattes and took everything in as we tried to figure out where to start. It was bigger than I had expected, but when I saw a banner for Sugarplum Sweets, I knew where I was going first.

"Come on," I squealed, grabbing Sebastian's hand and pulling him along.

The line was long but moved quickly as we waited, my stomach growling at the smell of delicious baked goods around us.

"Hi, welcome to Sugarplum Sweets. What can I get you?" The guy looked from me to Sebastian as I studied the options. There were new things I hadn't seen at the store when we went the other day, and now I was overwhelmed by too many options.

"We stopped by the other day and got these chocolate truffles," Sebastian said, already knowing that was what I had initially come to their booth for. "Do you by chance have any left?"

"Let me check." He bent down and rummaged under the table while the woman next to him bagged an order for another customer. "Hey, Andi, do we have more of the chocolate truffles?"

"I think we might have sold the last ones. Check the corner back there. If there aren't any, then we're completely sold out."

I chewed my nails anxiously while we watched him go through them and return empty-handed.

"Sorry, it looks like we're sold out of those. I have some coconut truffles if you're interested?"

Sebastian looked from the guy whose nametag read Zach, then to me, asking what I wanted to do. I shrugged and tried not to pout like a baby. I had my heart set on those truffles, so it was disappointing that they had already sold out of them.

"We'll take a box of coconut truffles," he confirmed, lifting his head as he scanned the rest of the boxes on the table. "We'll also take a box of maple pecan fudge, a dozen of the Santa sugar cookies, and a package of the chocolate-covered pretzels."

I pulled my purse around and reached for my wallet, but Sebastian put his hand out to stop me.

"Do you know when you guys will have the truffles again?" he asked as Zach rang him up.

"There's a chance we might have some at the shop, but I would have to call and check. If not, we should be fully stocked tomorrow morning. Are you guys staying in town?"

He handed Sebastian his card back and started bagging our stuff up.

"We're actually staying in a cabin up the mountain. We tried getting a hotel, but everything was sold out. This really nice guy overheard and offered us to stay at his place."

"Bert?" Zach asked as he passed the bag of goodies to Sebastian.

"Yeah, Bert. Really nice guy."

"He's one of the best," Andi said, smiling at us. "That cabin is pretty small, though. I'm surprised you guys haven't killed each other yet. The few times he's gone up with his wife, they've come back threatening to get divorced. You guys must have some holiday magic to survive up there."

"Oh, no. We're not together," I corrected, feeling my cheeks flame with embarrassment as everyone looked at me. "We're sharing the cabin but didn't know each other before that. Just both got stranded at the same time, and Bert was there to save the day."

"I'm sorry, I just assumed," Andi apologized. "But I'll give you even more credit for sharing the space with someone you don't know. Toss in an extra pack of fudge for them. They've earned it." Andi smiled at us, then turned to help the next customer as Zach grabbed another pack of fudge and added it to our bag.

We walked away and headed to the next booth, which happened to be Sugarplum Gifts. I immediately spotted the woman who had rung us up the other day when Sebastian purchased the tree topper and froze. I grabbed his arm and dragged him to the side, making sure I was out of sight before she could see me.

Twenty
Sebastian

"What's wrong?" I asked as Brynlee pulled me to the side and hid behind one of the lit-up Christmas trees.

"It's that woman who helped us the other day," she whispered, still crouched.

I lifted my head to get a look before she yanked me back.

"She's going to see you!"

"Why are we hiding from her?" I stood in front of Brynlee so my back was to the people walking past, shielding her from being seen.

"I don't know." She shrugged her shoulders, aggravated. "I don't know if my dream is making me react this way, but something deep inside is telling me to hide from her."

"Are you worried she's also trying to kill you?" There was enough humor in my voice to let her know I was teasing. I wasn't trying to make light of the situation and disregard how she felt, but I wanted to help her calm down so we could talk it out and find out why she was having such a reaction to a woman she didn't know.

"Very funny," she hissed, her lips pulled tight to keep the smile from gracing them as she playfully shoved my chest.

"I mean, there's a slight possibility she might be. You did buy the tree topper that reminded her of her cousin. Maybe she's got it out for you now."

"I didn't buy it, *you* did."

"Yeah, but she knew it was for you."

"Technicality," she muttered, looking past me to see the woman.

"Want to know what I think?" I asked, shoving my hands into my pockets.

"That she has more motives to kill me than you did?"

"No." I shook my head and looked at her until she finally met my gaze.

"Okay, what do you think?"

I took a deep breath and steadied myself before replying. She was already freaked out about seeing the woman, so I didn't want to make it worse. But I also wanted her to find whatever closure she needed, even if that meant she had to do something she didn't want to.

"I think that she reminds you of your past, and that's why you're afraid to talk to her. The connection you two share with the tree topper might be completely coincidental, but it could also be fate bringing you guys together for a reason."

She chewed her lip nervously as she looked from me back to the booth where the woman was.

"What am I supposed to do?"

"Let's go over and see what happens. We don't have to say anything to her until you're ready."

"What would I say to her? I wouldn't even have any idea how to start."

"Easy. You tell her that something about the tree topper reminded you of your childhood and go from there. You guys talk about timelines and put together the pieces to see if there's any connection or if it's just two people with a special memory of the same tree topper. It doesn't mean it was one of a kind and no one else ever had the same one. But we won't know anything unless you talk to her."

She pulled her shoulders back and then let them fall as she sighed heavily.

"Okay. Let's go talk to her."

Twenty-One
Brynlee

"I'm so nervous," I hissed under my breath as we approached the table. A few people were looking at ornaments, but there was an open space at the end where Sebastian guided me with his hand on my lower back. I took comfort from his touch and fought the urge to turn and run away.

I lowered my head and picked up a snow globe, pretending to study the intricate detail inside as the woman talked to the couple beside us. I wanted to be invisible and observe her, but I knew that wouldn't get me the answers I needed.

"Hello, I'm Hadley. Let me know if you have any questions."

I nodded my head, but my mouth was too dry to speak.

"We will, thank you," Sebastian replied for me, his hand still splayed across my lower back.

My palms were starting to sweat, so I put the snow globe down and turned to walk away. I couldn't do this. There was too much riding on the hopes that this random woman might know something about my past, and I couldn't stand the thought of how disappointed I would be if Sebastian were wrong about this being fate.

His arms wrapped around me in a hug as he braced himself against me, not allowing me to get past him.

"You can do this," he whispered in my ear. "I'm here if you need me."

I nodded but gave myself a few seconds before turning to the woman again. The couple beside us had left, leaving Sebastian and me as the only ones at the table.

"Was there anything specific you were looking for?" she asked, looking between us before recognition sparked in her eyes.

"We're actually just out doing some window shopping," Sebastian answered for me, but I could feel her eyes on me and knew she was thinking the same thing I was when I looked into hers.

I had seen those eyes before.

A long silence stretched between us as we stared at each other, a million unanswered questions floating between us.

"I'm sorry," she apologized, finally looking away and shaking her head. "I didn't mean to stare. You just… your eyes. They remind me—"

"Of my mom?" I offered, my voice cracking with emotion.

She lifted her hand to her mouth and blinked away the tears forming in her eyes.

"Are you… Are you Maggie?" she asked, a trail of wetness sliding down her cheeks.

I opened my mouth to say no, that wasn't my name, but stopped. In my dream, the woman holding me started to say a name, but I woke up before she could get it out. It began with Ma, but that was all I could grab before it ended.

"Maybe?" I replied uncertainly. "They called me Megan

while I was in the system, but I always hated that name, so I changed it to Brynlee once I was out on my own. I don't know what my real name was."

"Foster care?" Her eyes widened as more tears filled them.

A few people approached the table but didn't seem to notice what was happening between us.

"I'm sorry, I didn't mean to do this right now," I apologized, though I hadn't technically done anything.

"No, it's okay." She looked at them, then at her watch. "Will you guys be around for a while? I have my lunch break in twenty minutes. Maybe we can sit down and talk over a quick meal?"

I nodded quickly.

"Okay, perfect. I can meet you guys in the food court. Do you know where it is?"

"We passed by it on our way in," Sebastian said. "We'll grab a table and wait for you there."

"I look forward to it."

She smiled and turned her attention to the other customers as I forced my legs to walk away. My mind was racing with the things I wanted to ask her. Twenty minutes felt like forever, yet I was grateful for the opportunity to find out who I was.

Twenty-Two

Brynlee

It had been forty minutes, and we hadn't seen any sign of Hadley. I fidgeted under the table, worried she had changed her mind and decided not to come. Sebastian had done his best to keep me calm, but it was useless. I was getting ready to leave when I saw her frantically rushing our way.

"I'm so sorry," she rushed out, taking a seat at the table. "There was a scheduling error, and two people showed up instead of one. Instead of this being my lunch break, I am officially off for the rest of the day, which means we don't have to rush anything now."

"It's okay," I replied, meaning it. I was just thankful she had shown up.

"There are so many things I want to ask," she said with a soft smile. "But first, we should get some food. What are you guys in the mood for?"

My stomach had been turned upside down ever since I saw her at the booth, so nothing sounded good to me. I knew I needed to eat something, but I couldn't think about that when there was so much I needed to ask her.

"I was thinking pizza sounded good. What do you think, Brynlee?" Sebastian offered, his hand gently squeezing my knee.

He knew pizza was one of my favorite foods, so I appreciated that he was taking the lead.

"That works for me, thank you."

"I love pizza," Hadley said, pulling her wallet out of her purse. "Just let me know what you guys want, and I'll go grab it."

"Actually, I was going to check out the menu and see what sounded good. Why don't I go place the order and give you ladies a chance to talk?" Sebastian offered.

"Are you sure?"

"I don't mind at all. I already know what Brynlee likes, but what can I get for you?"

"I'll have a slice of the Hawaiian, please."

She slid her credit card out and tried to hand it to him, but he refused.

"Thank you, but it's my treat. Would you like something to drink?"

"Diet Coke, please."

"I'll be back." He winked at me and then walked off to get our food.

"I haven't stopped thinking about you since you came into the store the other day," Hadley said softly, resting her hands in front of her on the table. "Something about you made me feel like I knew you. I couldn't put my finger on what it was and just thought maybe I was emotional because of the tree topper."

"I had a dream about it that night," I admitted, looking into her eyes that felt so familiar. "I don't know where I was in my dream, but I was sitting on someone's lap, and they were bouncing me. We were looking at the tree, and I remember there being a lot of yelling around us. I don't know who was holding me, but I remember them telling her to be careful. Maybe a kid?"

Her face softened as she looked at me.

"I was holding you. We were at your house, and my mom and your mom were fighting."

"Did my mom come take me from you?"

She nodded.

"I was young. I was ten, and you were three, but she was still nervous I might drop you. But I loved showing you the tree. It was my favorite thing when your face would light up. Everything was so magical for you. That was our last Christmas together."

"Why?" I asked, even though deep down I knew. "Is that when my parents decided to give me up?"

She pulled her head back in shock and shook it.

"No, that wasn't it at all. Brynlee, your mother loved you so much. I never knew your dad. She raised you by herself."

"Then why did I end up in foster care?" A tear slid down my cheek as her eyes filled with them.

"I don't know what all happened," she said softly. "A lot of things were kept from me because I was just a kid. But your mom didn't give you up. She was killed in a car accident."

I lowered my head in my hands and cried.

"No one knew if you were with her when it happened. The police looked everywhere to see if you had been ejected from the car. They sent out search parties but couldn't find anything. But my mom didn't believe it. She told them to keep looking. She demanded they check in with the guy your mom had been dating. That was what she and your mom had been fighting over at Christmas. She knew he wasn't a good guy, but your mom wouldn't listen. She moved you guys in with him a few weeks later, and the accident happened right after that."

I took a deep breath and slowly released it as Sebastian returned with our food and set it on the table.

"By the time my mom got the police to look into him, it was weeks after the accident. When they went to question him, he was already gone. He skipped town, and no one heard anything about him after that. My mom figured he must have freaked out and left you somewhere because he couldn't take care of a child and didn't want the responsibility. He was a known drug user and probably didn't want to draw the attention of law enforcement."

I covered my mouth with my hand as I sobbed.

"We looked for you for years, Brynlee. We checked every single children's home for a three-year-old little girl named Maggie. No one had any record of you."

"That's because they had me down as a four-year-old named Megan."

Twenty-Three
Sebastian

"How are you feeling?" I asked as Brynlee rolled over and wiped the sleep away from her eyes.

"Like it was all a dream."

"A good one, or one of the ones you write stories about?" I teased, pulling her closer to my body.

"A good one, though I still cannot believe I have a cousin and that I got to meet her. It blows my mind. And speaking of stories, I have two days to finish my manuscript, or my ass is grass."

"I'm sorry for derailing the day yesterday and tying it up so you didn't get a chance to write."

I hadn't intended to pull her away for so long, but I also hadn't expected her to find her long-lost family.

"Oh, no. Please don't apologize. I'm grateful for everything you did for me yesterday. I can't even begin to thank you enough. Although, it still boggles my mind that I'm really only twenty-seven, not twenty-eight as I thought. I can't help but wonder what else Hadley knows about my life."

"Have you given any thought to her invite to join her and her mother for dinner on Christmas Eve?"

She sighed heavily, digging her head deeper into my chest. I kissed the top of it and gave her a moment.

"I don't know. I want to go, but I'm nervous."

"It's okay to feel that way."

"It's just a lot, all at once. You know? Like, I don't know how much more I can take right now before my head spins off into another universe."

"Well, I'm here to help however I can," I offered, squeezing her gently.

"Want to write my book for me?" She lifted her head and grinned at me.

"Can I add some romance to it?"

"I don't think my character will enjoy it too much." She scrunched her nose.

"You never know. She might love it."

She laughed lightly, pulling away from me and rolling out of the bed.

"I need to take a shower and wake up, or I'll never get the day started."

I nodded, stretching out in the now empty bed.

"Wanna join me?" she offered, pulling her shirt over her head and tossing it to the floor.

I was up on my feet quicker than she could get to the bathroom door, wrapping my arms around her waist and loving the feel of her breasts against my arm. My cock immediately hardened, desperate to be inside her again.

She reached in and turned on the water, giving it a few minutes to warm up as we stripped off our clothes and got in.

I knew she wanted to actually shower, but that didn't stop the dirty thoughts that were racing through my head.

"I have a lot of writing to get done today," she warned, raising an eyebrow as she felt my dick poke her in the butt as I stood behind her.

"Then I guess we should be quick," I teased, nibbling the bottom of her ear as my hands roamed over her breasts, brushing against her nipples.

"Think you can manage to fuck me thoroughly from behind while I wash my hair?"

"Are you asking for a multi-tasking quickie?" I arched an eyebrow.

"You bet I am. We're both horny with pressing deadlines. You have a better idea?"

I rubbed my thumb across my jaw, remembering I still needed to shave at some point.

"I think I do."

I handed her the shampoo bottle from the shelf and lowered myself between her legs as the water dripped over my head. She squirted some into her hand and then gasped as I pressed an open-mouthed kiss to her pussy.

Her legs parted the best they could without her losing her balance as I wrapped my hands around her thighs to hold her in place as I devoured her. My tongue slid through her wetness as I teased her clit, nipping and sucking eagerly.

"Ouch!" she muttered, leaning back further into the water.

"Too much?" I asked, barely pulling my mouth away from her sex.

"Keep going," she panted. "I got shampoo in my eye, but it's worth it if you give me the orgasm that's building up."

I chuckled against her pussy and began licking and sucking again, driving her wild.

When I knew she was getting close to coming, I lifted one of her legs above my shoulder and pressed her body against the tiled wall to hold her steady. Then I inserted two fingers inside her, pumping in and out quickly as I sucked her clit to bring her over the edge.

"YES!" she moaned, digging her nails into my hair as the water rushed over my head. I kept sucking until I felt her pussy spasm against my tongue and her legs weakened.

I helped steady her, then handed her the bottle of tropical-scented body wash as if nothing had happened. She moved out of the water to give me a turn, her eyes traveling down to my raging hard-on. I grabbed my body wash from the shelf and poured some into my hand before lowering it to my cock and stroking it.

Brynlee watched as she washed her body, rubbing her loofah in odd patterns, clearly distracted by the show. I gripped my shaft harder, easing into a painfully slow speed as I turned my wrist and went back up.

She reached forward and replaced my hand with hers, rubbing me faster and harder than I had been.

"Brynlee," I warned, not ready to come yet.

"Then fuck me now. Hard and fast," she ordered, locking eyes with me.

I spun her around to face the wall as I brought her hips back to me. She leaned forward and braced her hands against it to hold herself up as I spread her legs with my foot and lined myself up at her entrance.

"Fuck," I groaned, letting my head fall back. "I don't have a condom in here."

"I'm on the pill," she assured me. "I haven't been with anyone in over a year and got tested at my annual check-up."

"I got checked right after the breakup. The results came through my email a few days ago. I'm clean."

"Okay, then fuck me. Please."

I didn't need to hear anything more as I lined myself up and slowly slid inside her. My eyes pinched closed as I gripped her hips tightly to keep from pounding into her and blowing my load right away.

"I just need a minute," I said, my voice hoarse.

"I'm very impatient," she teased, rocking her hips against me, her walls squeezing my cock harder.

"Fuck, Brynlee," I growled, pulling back and slamming into her. "I forgot how much you like when I pound into you."

She nodded and groaned, lifting her ass to let me go deeper.

I held onto her with everything I had and fucked her hard and rough, just the way she liked it.

Twenty-Four

Brynlee

"What's another word for strangulated?" I asked, leaning back against the headboard and rolling my head on my neck. We'd been writing for four hours straight, and while it was more comfortable than the table, I was still sore from sitting so long.

"Choked?" Sebastian offered, thinking about it as he pulled his mouth to the side. "Smothered? Restrained? Suppressed?"

"Are you looking up synonyms in Word, too?" I asked with a smile.

"Yeah. Nothing like that easily comes to mind for me. Now, if you'd asked for another word for cunnilingus, I could easily rattle those off, no problem."

"Hmmm. As tempting as that is, I don't think she's planning to murder this guy by having him go down on her."

"It could work. He could have his face buried in her pussy— much like mine was in yours earlier—and then she can do a triangle choke move and suffocate him to death," he offered.

"Do I even want to Google what triangle choke is?" I teased, giving him my best judgmental face.

"I'll show you later." He winked. "I need a writing break. Anything you feel like for dinner?"

He closed the lid of his laptop and set it on the table beside him as he got up.

"I'm good with whatever you feel like. I'm going to wrap up this chapter, and then I can come help you."

"It's okay. I got it, but thank you. Keep writing. You're getting so close to being done."

I looked down at the word count total in the bottom corner of the screen and sighed. I was ninety percent done and wanted to keep pushing through, but my brain was already feeling fried.

Sebastian went to start dinner when my phone started to ring. I had called Macy last night on our way back to the cabin, but she hadn't answered. I swiped my finger across the screen to answer it.

"Hey," I said, wondering if this conversation would be better over FaceTime.

"Hi! Sorry I missed your call last night."

"It's okay. Do you want to FaceTime?" I could hear the nervousness in my tone and knew she had picked up on it, too.

"Sure… Is everything okay? You didn't do anything to F.E. Tish, did you?" she whispered loudly.

"No," I assured her with a laugh as I pulled the phone away to press the button to turn on FaceTime. A second later, Macy's face filled my screen.

"There, that's much better," I said, happy to see my best friend. "How's it going?"

"Good. Busy. I always forget how hectic this time of year

gets for me. I was at my mom's house until after midnight last night helping her bake for the annual bake sale at her church. I was so exhausted, I practically slept the day away."

"I wish I were sleeping that much," I teased.

She made a sad face and smiled empathetically at me.

"How's it going with the deadline?"

"Pretty good. I got a lot done today but still have about 6,000 words left to write, with only a day and a half to do it."

"You've got this," she assured me. "And this book is going to be great. People already love this series, and your preorders have been soaring for this book. You're going to be the next New York Times bestselling author!"

"I seriously doubt that," I said with a laugh. "But I can't even think about that right now."

I glanced at the kitchen, wondering if Sebastian was listening to our conversation. It wasn't like I could go into another room to take the call unless I wanted to hide in the bathroom—which I didn't. And it was way too cold to go outside.

"Why do I feel like something else is going on that I don't know about?" She eyed me cautiously and then tried to mouth the words, *"are you fucking him."*

I shook my head and covered my mouth to try to hide the stupid grin on it.

"You are!" she exclaimed, clapping her hands.

I gave her a stern look and then checked again to see if Sebastian was paying attention to us.

"Stop it," I tried to hiss, this time drawing his eyes to me as he turned slightly and smirked.

My cheeks flamed red, and I knew she wasn't going to let this go. Her eyes widened as she tipped her head back, silently shaking her arms and stomping her feet. I gave her a few seconds to get it out of her system.

"This is amazing!" she finally said, already forgetting that he was in the same room. "Can I see him?"

"No." I raised my eyebrows in warning at her.

"Why not?" she whispered, coming closer to the screen. "Just walk around like you're getting something. I'll be quiet as a mouse."

"No. You're being ridiculous," I teased, rolling my eyes at her.

"Hey, Brynlee? Can you come help me in the kitchen?" Sebastian asked nonchalantly.

I had a feeling I knew what he was up to, but still got up and walked over to where he stood by the stove.

"What's up?" I asked, holding the phone against my chest. I had already flipped the camera from selfie mode so Macy didn't see my face but whatever the phone was aimed at, which happened to be Sebastian. I heard soft giggling on the other side and knew she was happy to get her way.

"I need your opinion on this spicy peanut sauce. I'm not sure it's *hot* enough."

He licked his lips and extended a spoon to me. I parted my lips and tasted it, noticing the way his eyes darkened as he watched.

"It's umm, it's good. Hot. Very hot."

"Good. Just the way I like it."

I nodded, unsure what else to say, as Macy giggled on the other end.

I glanced down at the phone now aimed at the ceiling, and found her bent over laughing.

"What are you laughing about?" I asked quietly, heading back to the bed as I debated hiding in the bathroom.

"I thought he said *penis* sauce." She laughed harder, a snort coming through.

My eyes widened, but not because of what she said, but because Sebastian casually walked over and plopped down on the bed beside me. He gently grabbed my hand and adjusted it so we were on the screen.

"I usually call that one something else," he said smoothly, bringing a fresh wave of crimson over her cheeks.

"Oh. My. God. *You're* F.E. Tish!"

"I am. But don't tell anyone. It'll ruin the illusion that I'm some old, grumpy woman who doesn't get enough sex, so I have to write about it in great detail." He winked.

"Has someone said that to you before?" I asked, turning to look at him while forgetting Macy was on the phone.

"Yeah. In a few reviews, as well as a handful of emails detailing how they knew it was true."

"They'll be shocked if they ever find out the truth," Macy said, pulling our attention back to her.

"Anyway," I said, hoping to change the subject. "This is Sebastian. Sebastian, this is my best friend, Macy."

"It's a pleasure to meet you," he said with a cheeky smile.

"I'm sure the pleasure is all Brynlee's," she teased. Now it was my turn to have my cheeks flush with color.

Thankfully, Sebastian let the comment slide and changed the conversation for me.

"So, are you ready for Christmas?" he asked, leaning back against the bed with his arms raised above his head as he relaxed for a few minutes.

"As ready as I'm going to be." She sighed heavily and then looked back at me. "Did you still want to FaceTime when we open our gifts from each other?"

"Yeah, as long as you have the time. You're busier than I am on Christmas, so it's your call."

"I was actually going to see if we could do Christmas Eve instead?" Her face fell, and I knew she thought she was disappointing me by not doing it on Christmas day. Sebastian squeezed my knee before getting up and checking on dinner.

"I'm not sure what my plans are yet," I said nervously, knowing now was as good of a time as any to tell her about Hadley. "I actually have some news I was calling to share with you last night."

"Okay… You're starting to worry me, though. What's wrong?"

"Nothing is *wrong*. But I might have accidentally stumbled upon a family member I never knew I had."

Her eyes nearly bulged out of her head.

"Sebastian and I went into town a few days ago and stopped in this gift shop. There was this beautiful tree topper there that I immediately fell in love with. I couldn't figure out why, but it felt like I had seen it before." I turned my phone and aimed it at the tree topper sitting on top of the tree. "Sebastian insisted on buying it for me, and the woman who rang me up told us a story about how it reminded her of her aunt and how much her cousin loved staring at it."

I took a deep breath and fought off the tears, but when I saw Sebastian watching me from the kitchen, I found the strength I needed to go on.

"I had a dream about it that night and just figured it was because I had felt so emotional about it at the store. But in the dream, I felt like it was real. Like I had been in that house before. I told Sebastian about it, and he thought it might be fate bringing closure to my past. I kinda blew that idea off and didn't think about it again until we went into town yesterday for the Frosty Fest. She was working a booth there, and when I looked into her eyes, something clicked."

"Oh my gosh," Macy whispered, leaning forward as she hung onto my every word.

"We ended up sitting down and talking with her for a while. It seems my mother hadn't abandoned me. She was killed in a car accident, and the guy she was dating turned me over to child protective services before fleeing town. He didn't know much about me, so he told them I was four and that my name was Megan. My aunt looked everywhere for me, but no one had any record of a three-year-old girl named Maggie."

"This is so crazy!" she gasped, shaking her head as we processed what I said. "So your name wasn't Megan, and you're actually a year younger than you thought?"

"So it seems. She offered to do one of those genetic testing kits with me so we could get confirmation."

"That's really nice of her. How old is she?"

"Thirty-four. She was only ten years old when I *vanished*."

"Wow. That's unbelievable, Bryn. How do you feel about all of this?"

I leaned back on the bed and thought about it.

"I don't know. Happy that I finally have some answers about my past. Sad that I spent so much of my life thinking my parents abandoned me when, in reality, my mom died, and I didn't even have a chance to grieve her. Confused about who my real dad was and why he was never in the picture. There's a ton of questions, and I just wish I had answers to them."

"Will you get to see her again while you're there? Can you sit down and see what else she knows?"

"She invited us to dinner at her house on Christmas Eve. Her mom will be there too. Or, I guess I should say, *my aunt*. It still feels weird to say that."

"Are you going to go?"

I shrugged. I hadn't decided yet, but deep down, I felt something saying I should.

"Well, you have a day to decide. I'm sure they would love to see you. I can't even imagine how your aunt must feel, knowing that not only are you alive, but you're well and in town. What are the chances something like that would happen?"

"They're pretty good when it's fate," Sebastian answered from the kitchen. "I'm going to push her to finish her manuscript on time, and then maybe I can convince her to go to dinner. I mean, I think it's pretty selfish that she's going to deprive me of a home-cooked meal just because she's nervous to meet a woman who will smother her in hugs the second she sees her." He winked as he crossed the room and joined me on the bed again.

"Is she getting anything out of this deal, you know, with her being so selfish and all?" Macy teased. "Maybe she needs a *bigger* incentive."

Sebastian refused to look at me as he stared directly into the camera and pinned Macy with a look.

"Trust me, my *penis* sauce is plenty of motivation for her." He winked, wrapping his arm around my shoulders as Macy's jaw dropped.

Twenty-Five
Sebastian

It was two days until Christmas, and I was feeling the anxiety rolling off Brynlee as she worked on finishing her book before her deadline tomorrow. We'd done sprinting sessions throughout the morning, but she'd skipped lunch to keep going. She was on a roll, and I didn't want to do anything to stop it.

I was surprised by how far I'd gotten with my own manuscript. It seemed like having a writing buddy—just someone to hold me accountable—really increased my productivity. If I kept going at this rate, I would have my book ready a few days before my deadline.

The sky darkened as an evening storm rolled in, bringing another cold front. I put on my coat and gloves, then pulled a beanie over my head before heading out to the garage to fetch more firewood. We were nearing the end of the pile, which meant I would need to get out here and chop more wood. But for now, we had enough to get us through the night.

When I walked into the cabin, Brynlee was standing at the table, staring down at her computer.

"It's done," she said proudly, a huge grin on her face. "I just sent it off to my editor."

"Congratulations!" I set the wood on the floor beside me and pulled her in for a hug. "I'm so proud of you!"

"Thank you. I couldn't have done it without you pushing me and joining me for writing sessions."

"I enjoyed them too." I hugged her tighter, not wanting to let go. "We should do something to celebrate."

"Like what?" She nuzzled her cheek against my chest.

"Well, I would offer to take you to dinner, but the weather has gotten bad tonight, so I don't think that's a good idea. I can make you dinner, though."

"You don't have to cook for me."

"We've been together in this cabin for ten days, Brynlee. Three meals a day most days is almost thirty meals we've shared. You should know by now that I enjoy cooking for you. It's never a problem for me."

She leaned up and kissed my cheek.

"Thank you. I do enjoy your cooking. Even your *spicy penis sauce.*"

I tickled her sides and kissed her forehead before releasing her. I grabbed the firewood and put it away after tossing a few logs in.

"So, is there anything you feel like for dinner?"

"Pizza sounds good," she said lightly, joining me in the kitchen.

"You know I can make more than frozen pizza, right? This is your celebration dinner."

"I know, but I really love pizza and wine."

"Are you sure?"

She nodded and grabbed a bottle of red wine from the counter while I pulled out one of her favorite pizzas from the freezer and preheated the oven.

"I was thinking about going into town tomorrow," she said quietly, peeling the foil off the bottle.

"Yeah?"

"I want to go shopping. For Christmas gifts." She stopped what she was doing and stared at the counter for a second. "For my family."

My heart tightened at the emotion in her words.

"I think that's a wonderful idea. We can get up early and head in. Maybe grab breakfast at the cute little café we saw?"

"And definitely grab some lattes from Sam. He's so nice, and those drinks were amazing."

"Deal. We'll make a day of it."

"Okay," she said shakily, her hand trembling as she tried to pour the wine.

I stood behind her and guided her with my hand so she didn't spill.

"I've got you, Brynlee. Whatever you need, I've always got you."

"I wanted to look for a new dress, too. Something I can wear to dinner tomorrow night." She turned in my arms and looked up at me. "Will you go with me to meet my aunt?"

"I wouldn't miss it." I kissed the tip of her nose and held her for a few minutes, falling harder for her by the second.

Twenty-Six

Brynlee

"Are you sure this one is okay?" I asked, studying myself in the mirror as Sebastian nodded his head.

"I love all of them, so it's whatever you feel the most comfortable in."

"I feel anything but comfortable," I muttered, rubbing my hands down the maroon-colored sweater dress. "Why did I decide to do this? I should call and tell Hadley I can't make it after all."

"You're just nervous, and that's to be expected. But remember how nervous you were about talking to Hadley? Then you guys sat down, and everything was fine. It's going to be the same tonight. It's just Hadley and your aunt. I promise she's going to be so excited to see you."

I chewed the inside of my cheek. I knew he was right, but that didn't stop the butterflies swarming through my stomach.

"What time is it?" I asked, remembering that a lot of the stores would be closing early today since it was Christmas Eve.

"Ten thirty."

I nodded and took one more look in the mirror before going back to the dressing room to change. When I came out, I found Sebastian in the jewelry department, looking at something in a display case.

He looked up, spotted me heading his way, and shook his head, pointing a finger for me to turn around. I gave him a confused look that matched the pointed one he gave me. I laughed and then redirected myself to the display of hats and scarves.

I wanted to get him something, but I hadn't figured out what yet. I looked at Frosty Fest, but it was hard to shop for anyone while my head was spinning after meeting Hadley. This was my last chance to get a gift, and the clock was ticking.

I went around the corner, relieved when I saw stuff that he would like. I grabbed a pair of leather gloves, a thicker beanie than the one he had been wearing, and a scarf that would look good with the leather jacket I had seen him wear a few times when he wasn't wearing his winter coat.

"Find anything good?" he asked, startling me as I tossed my sweater over the stuff in my cart so he couldn't see it.

"A few things. You?"

He nodded with a smug grin on his face.

"Did you want to look here for something for your aunt and Hadley?" he offered, looking around the store.

We had been to Waldon's several times for groceries, but I was still surprised by how much other stuff they had.

"I have no idea what to get them," I admitted.

"How about some scented candles? Maybe a nice selection of chocolates? Like one of those boxes that have a mix of everything?"

My eyes lit up at *chocolate*.

"Oooh! If we have time, we can make it over to Sugarplum Sweets. I can grab some stuff for them there."

"You just want to go so you can get more truffles for *yourself.*"

"Maybe." I shrugged. "But if you're nice to me, I'll share them with you."

"Deal."

I insisted that we go to separate registers to pay for our stuff; that way, he couldn't see what I was buying for him. We hadn't talked about whether to exchange gifts since we'd be spending Christmas together, but I wanted to get him something regardless. We loaded our bags into the back of the truck, then stopped for a latte before heading down the sidewalk to Sugarplum Sweets.

When we walked in, the sweet aroma of baked goods filled the air and made my mouth water.

"I could seriously live here," I joked, though part of me was serious.

"I can see if they have any job openings," he offered playfully.

"No way. I would eat more than I would sell. My ass has already doubled in size in the eleven days I've been in Sugarplum Falls. I can't risk it getting any bigger."

He lifted the bottom of my coat and leaned to get a better look at my ass.

"I think it's just fine. In fact, I like a nice, plump ass. Why don't we get two orders of truffles?"

I swatted his arm as we walked to the register.

"Hey! It's nice to see you two again," Andi, the woman we'd met at Frosty Fest, said. "I'm down to my last few boxes of truffles if you want them."

"Yes, please," I begged, pressing my hands together.

She laughed and went around the counter to grab them from the shelf.

"Anything else, or just the truffles?"

"I'm, umm… I'm meeting my aunt for the first time tonight, and I wanted to take something for her and my cousin, but I don't know what they would like," I explained, feeling stupid. "I know that's an odd thing to say, but do you have any premade gift baskets or something like that?"

"Come with me. I think I have the perfect idea."

I followed her through the store as she pointed out a few different premade sets she had. Nothing was screaming "perfect gift," which made my heart sink further down my chest.

Andi's eyes softened as she smiled sadly at me.

"Why don't we put together a basket instead of going with the premade ones?" she suggested.

"I don't want to make any extra work for you."

"It's fine. I promise. Zach is in the back with Autumn, working on some orders that are being picked up soon, but they can come up front if someone else comes in. I'm all yours, so let's make the best basket your heart desires."

I smiled and allowed her to lead me through the store, going over all the options and making sure we didn't pick anything with nuts, just in case either had a food allergy.

By the time we were done, Sebastian was eating a coconut truffle that Zach had given him while Andi put together two custom baskets for me. I had no idea what my aunt and cousin liked, but everyone loved chocolate. Right?

Twenty-Seven
Brynlee

Sebastian rang the doorbell and stepped back, keeping his hand on my lower back protectively. We had time to go back to the cabin and get ready before dinner, but I'd spent that time stressing over meeting my aunt. The door opened, and Hadley greeted us on the other side.

"I'm so glad you guys could make it," she said happily, holding the door open for us.

"Thank you for the invite," I replied, clutching the gifts tighter against my body.

Sebastian guided me in and then took the gifts and my purse so I could take my coat off. I hung it beside his on the coat rack, then rubbed my hands together to ward off the cold spreading through me.

Before I could say anything, a woman appeared in the doorway, and my heart dropped. I blinked quickly, trying to force the tears away. She lifted her hands to her face, her eyes filling with tears.

"You look just like her," she whispered, stepping closer but unsure whether to hug me.

I nodded, my jaw trembling.

"Can I?" she asked, extending her arms.

I nodded again, and then her arms were around me, holding me tight as if she were worried I would disappear again. I returned the hug, burying my head in her neck as I cried harder.

I heard sniffling and knew we weren't the only two crying. At some point, the door was closed behind us, and Sebastian and Hadley had left to give us some privacy.

My aunt pulled back slightly, her hands gently gripping my arms as she studied my face.

"You're so beautiful. Still the little girl I remember, but now a grown woman."

"I don't remember much from my childhood," I admitted, lowering my head. I felt bad that I wasn't able to return any compliments, but I had no idea what she used to look like.

"I'm so sorry, Mag—Brynlee." She pressed her lips into a line as she corrected herself. "I know I can't change the past or what happened to you, but I am so happy to have you here with us tonight. Thank you for coming."

We joined Hadley and Sebastian in the kitchen, and it took me a few minutes to take everything in. The house was large and beautifully decorated, and I wondered if Hadley did it herself or if she and her mom did it together. Or maybe a significant other? We hadn't had enough time to talk about what their family looked like, only that she assured me it would be just the two of them for dinner tonight.

"Your house is beautiful," I said, smiling at my cousin.

"Thank you. It's bigger than what I need for just me, but the idea when I bought it was that someday I would have a family to fill it."

"You're only thirty-four, Had. There's still time for that to happen," my aunt assured her, squeezing her shoulders gently before approaching Sebastian.

"I'm sorry, I got so caught up in seeing Brynlee that I didn't introduce myself. I'm Beth," she said, extending her hand.

"Sebastian. It's a pleasure to meet you. Thank you so much for inviting us for dinner."

"Please believe me when I say that it's our pleasure." My aunt squeezed his hand and turned to look at me. "I've waited so long for this day."

We followed Hadley to the long wooden table in the corner of the room next to two large windows. A gorgeous cream lace runner ran down the middle with several bottles of wine. It looked simple but fancy at the same time, the perfect blend of holiday festive without being too extravagant.

Sebastian pulled my chair out and then sat beside me, squeezing my knee the way he always did when he knew I was nervous.

Hadley brought in dishes and set them on the table as her mom helped her.

"I hope it's okay, but I made Christmas dinner the way your mom used to," she said softly, a wave of uncertainty flashing across her face. "My mom helped me. We thought it might…"

She sat down, and her shoulders slumped.

"It's perfect," I assured her quickly. "Thank you so much. I'll admit that I don't remember much about the past, but I'm so touched by the thoughtfulness you both put into making dinner special for me tonight."

The smell of oven-roasted turkey made my mouth water as I looked over the items spread out on the table. There were mashed potatoes and green bean casserole, both of which were staples with Macy's family, so I'd gotten used to having them with holiday meals. But then there were the most delicious-looking bread rolls that grabbed my attention, and I found myself reaching for one in the basket before I could stop myself.

My aunt's eyes lit up as she watched me and I wondered what it must feel like for her. I didn't remember any of my family, but she clearly remembered the first three years of my life before I was put into the system.

"Those are your mom's recipe," she said softly. "She couldn't get you to eat much of anything else on Christmas other than mashed potatoes and her rolls."

I held it in my hands and stared at it as if I were given a piece of her.

Everyone began filling their plates while Sebastian leaned in to whisper in my ear.

"Are you okay?"

I nodded, too afraid to speak and have everyone hear the emotion lodged in my throat.

"Would you like some turkey?" he offered.

I smiled and accepted the platter he handed me. Soon, my plate was filled with food, and my stomach growled.

"So, how long have you two been together?" my aunt asked, catching both of us off guard.

"Oh. Um." I turned to look at him, panic in my eyes.

"Well, we… It's a long story."

"What she means to say is that we haven't defined our relationship yet," Sebastian answered for me. "But I've always believed in doing things the right way. So, to make sure there's no confusion on where we stand, I have a question for you Brynlee."

He turned sideways in his seat to face me, then grabbed my hand and held it in his.

"Brynlee, will you be my girlfriend?"

My mouth fell open, but not because I was shocked by his question—I just hadn't expected him to be so cute with how he asked me.

"I would love to," I said happily. "But I'm not sure how this will work since we don't even have a placc to live."

"You're homeless?" Beth gasped, clutching her hand to her chest while the wine sloshed in the glass in her other hand.

"No," I laughed. "I mean, I guess maybe? It's hard to explain, but we don't live here. We were both traveling through Sugarplum Falls when we got stranded by the first blizzard. We didn't know each other before that. Just two strangers forced to share a cabin because there was nowhere else to go."

"But it's been the best eleven days of my life," Sebastian said softly. "I came through town not having a plan or any direction, Brynlee. So trust me when I say I will follow you wherever you go. Wherever *you* want to call home."

"Are you planning to leave soon?" Hadley asked, her voice barely above a whisper.

I swallowed hard, not wanting to have this conversation with them right now because the plan had been to leave town as soon as the roads were clear. I hadn't expected to find my family or fall in lo—. I exhaled heavily as the weight of everything sat on my shoulders.

Twenty-Eight

Sebastian

My *girlfriend* had been quiet most of the night after dinner. It still felt weird to be able to call her that, but I was over the moon that she had said yes. I hadn't meant to put her on the spot with her family wanting to know if she was going to be in town for a while, but I also hated not knowing what would be next once the roads cleared. We hadn't talked about it, but with each day that passed, I fell harder, and it became impossible to think of *not* spending my time with her anymore.

I helped clean up dinner while Brynlee and her aunt went to the living room to talk. The night had been pleasant, and I could see her relax more around them as it went on.

"Would you mind helping me take the tray of cookies and eggnog to the living room?" Hadley asked, closing the fridge.

"Not at all."

I grabbed the tray she pointed to and followed her to where the girls were sitting. I set it on the coffee table, then took a seat on the sectional next to Brynlee.

"How many books have you written?" Beth asked, leaning in to snag a cookie from the tray, the proudest smile reaching across her face.

"So far, three, if you count the one I just finished."

"I can't believe we have an author in our family. That's so cool," Hadley said. "Are they steamy romance?"

Brynlee shook her head and grinned.

"No, no romance. I write thrillers, but I do have a favorite steamy romance author I can recommend if you're interested."

"Ooh, tell me. I just finished a series I love and need something else to get obsessed with. You know, single girl life—gotta get all of my action from smutty books."

"Have you read F.E. Tish?" Brynlee asked coyly. I knew she wouldn't blow my cover, but honestly, I was getting tired of trying to keep it.

"YES!! Oh my gosh! I LOVE her books! They're so good and the perfect combo of plot and spice. I mean, I've found out I have kinks I never would have imagined." Hadley winced and looked over at her mom. "Sorry, mom. Pretend you didn't hear that."

"I'll pretend if you pretend that I don't come in and borrow your books when I know you're done with them. And I'll agree, I love F.E. Tish's books."

Brynlee looked discreetly at me, and I nodded my head.

"Do you have your paperbacks handy?" she asked Hadley.

"Yeah, they're on my bookshelf. Do you want to see them?"

"Yes, please."

Hadley got up and grabbed a stack, then sat them on the coffee table in front of Brynlee.

"Do you have a pen?" Brynlee asked.

"Yeah…" Hadley furrowed her brow in confusion as she grabbed one from the end table. "Here you go."

"Thanks." Brynlee turned and handed it to me. "Would you do the honor of signing her books?"

"It would be my pleasure." I took the pen and looked up to find Hadley and Beth staring at me in disbelief.

"YOU are F.E. Tish?" Hadley squealed, plopping down on the couch beside her mom.

"I am."

"I thought you were a woman," Beth said with a soft laugh.

"Honestly, I thought the same. Hell, I was convinced he was a murderer and was going to kill me in the cabin." Brynlee shrugged.

"Why would you think that?" Beth asked, brows pinched together.

"She watches way too much true crime," I answered for Brynlee. "Are you sure you want me to sign these?" I didn't want to assume it was okay and then ruin her books.

"Are you really F.E. Tish?" Hadley asked.

"Yes. Do you want me to show you my credentials?"

"No," she laughed. "Your signature is more than enough. If you weren't dating my cousin, I would ask you to lick them or something."

"Hadley," Beth scolded, shoving her leg playfully. "Don't be gross."

"What?" She laughed harder. "I'm just saying, if F.E. Tish were single and at a book signing—women would be asking him to do more than lick the pages. Probably some of the men, too."

"That's why I don't do signings," I joked.

I got to work signing the books while the girls chatted. It was nice being around her family, even if she didn't know them yet. They had that kind of natural bond where they all seemed to gravitate to each other, and the awkwardness that was there earlier had completely disappeared.

I put them back into a neat pile and set the pen beside them.

"Thank you for signing those," Hadley said. "Knowing that you don't do any signings, I feel like that is such a special gift."

"Not a problem. It was my pleasure."

"Speaking of gifts," Brynlee said, standing up. "We brought a few."

She went over to the bench where we had left them earlier and handed one to her cousin and the other to her aunt.

"Thank you so much," Hadley said, smiling before pulling the paper off.

"Yes, thank you. You guys didn't need to get us anything. Having you here is gift enough." Beth smiled warmly.

As soon as they saw the treats inside, their eyes lit up.

"You know the way to my heart," Hadley said, digging through the goodies in her basket.

"I thought that was through smut?" her mom teased.

"Well, that too. Now I have something to snack on while I read. Thank you so much, you guys."

"You're very welcome," Brynlee said, leaning into my side as I draped an arm over her shoulders.

"This is a wonderful assortment. Thank you so much," Beth said, leaning over to hug Brynlee. "I have a gift for you, too."

She set her basket on the table and went over to the tree in the corner of the room.

"It's not much, but I wanted you to have it." Beth handed Brynlee a keepsake box with a red ribbon tied around it.

I pulled my arm away to give her space as she opened it.

"Is this…" Brynlee asked, covering her mouth as tears filled her eyes. She held the photo up, and Beth nodded.

"That's you and your mom at Christmas. That was the last time I saw either of you."

She continued to stare at it, the tears running down her cheeks, but she didn't bother to wipe them away.

"Those are all of the photos I had of you when you were little, and some I had of your mom throughout the years. I thought you might want to have them."

"This is amazing, thank you."

Brynlee continued looking through the photos, showing me them as she went. Her aunt told her when each one was taken and had taken the time to write as many details about each one as she could on the back of them.

It was getting late, but I didn't want to rush Brynlee while she was spending time with her family. I knew if we didn't get going soon, we would have a hard time getting back up the mountain once the roads froze again.

"We should get going," she said, as if reading my mind.

I noticed the sad look on her aunt's face when she said it.

"Yeah, the road back to the cabin will be pure ice soon," I agreed.

"Oh. Of course." Beth stood, and Hadley joined her, both looking disappointed.

"What are your plans tomorrow?" Hadley asked, looking between us.

Brynlee looked up at me, unsure how to answer.

"I don't think we have any. Just opening presents in the morning," I answered.

"Well, if it's not too much trouble to make it into town, I would love to have you guys join us for dinner at my house," Beth offered. "We don't dress up, and it's nothing fancy. We open gifts in the morning and then spend the day in our pajamas, eating cookies. You're welcome to join us."

Brynlee opened her mouth to say something but closed it before she could. She was hesitating, but I didn't know why.

"Thanks for the invite. I'll make sure Brynlee lets you know in the morning."

We said goodbye, and then I guided her to the truck, not pushing her to tell me what was going on until she was ready.

Twenty-Nine
Brynlee

"Good morning. Merry Christmas," Sebastian said as I rolled over and faced him.

"Merry Christmas," I whispered, still waking up.

Last night had been a late night by the time we got back from Hadley's. I was still wound up from the thoughts spinning in my head that I hadn't been able to fall asleep until sometime after midnight.

"How are you feeling this morning?" His finger brushed the side of my cheek lightly.

"I'm okay. How are you?"

"Happy to be waking up in bed next to my girlfriend. Unless you've changed your mind about that."

We hadn't talked about it last night, and I was hoping we wouldn't have to discuss it today either. But the truth was that the roads were starting to clear, and soon, we wouldn't have an excuse to stay *stuck* in this cabin together anymore.

"I haven't," I assured him with a shake of my head. "But we still need to talk and figure out what happens next."

"I know. We'll make time for that, I promise. But right now, I want to give you your Christmas present, then make breakfast because I'm starving."

"You didn't need to get me a gift," I said, sitting up next to him.

"I wanted to."

He reached over his side of the bed and pulled up a box wrapped in the shimmery silver paper I had seen him buy at Waldon's yesterday.

"I have a gift for you, too." I got up, walked to the small closet by the door, and pulled out a gift bag.

I sat down next to him to exchange gifts, smiling at each other as we started opening them.

He pulled the tissue paper out and grinned when he spotted the beanie.

"You knew how cold my head has been up here, didn't you?"

"I did. I wasn't sure whether you would like that one, but if not, we can go into town and exchange it."

"It's perfect." He pulled it onto his head, his smile beaming at me.

"It looks great. But then again, you could wear a paper bag on your head and it would still look great."

"Right back at you, baby." He winked and pulled out the gloves, admiring them before slipping them on. "These are awesome, Brynlee. Thank you so much."

"You're welcome," I answered, peeling the ribbon off the box and tearing the paper. It looked so pretty that I didn't want to mess it up.

He wrapped the scarf around his neck and watched as I opened the lid to the box and found several smaller boxes inside. Each one was wrapped and had a number written on it.

"Go in order," he said, smiling as I picked up the box marked 1.

I peeled off the paper and found a long jewelry-shaped box. I raised my eyebrows, but he just nodded for me to keep going. I opened it slowly and found a charm bracelet inside with one charm on it.

"It's for you to write your own story, Brynlee," he said softly. "I picked the cabin charm because it felt like the place where everything started. The other stuff might not have happened if we hadn't been stuck together in this cabin." He shrugged and grinned a crooked smile.

"Thank you, Sebastian. It's beautiful, and I love the meaning behind it."

The rest of the boxes were smaller but different sizes, which piqued my curiosity. I grabbed the next box and opened it, finding another charm inside.

"It's a book because that's what drew us together. What were the odds that two amazing authors would get stuck in a blizzard with nowhere else to go?"

I laughed and added the charm to the bracelet, admiring it.

Box 3 was bigger, but when I opened it, there was another smaller box inside. I shook my head and opened it, finding a candy charm.

"For your love of truffles."

"Did you get a charm with a giant butt?" I teased. "I'll need one to show what all of those truffles have done to me."

"Nope. Your ass is fine. If you want, I can show you just how much I love it with some special attention after breakfast."

"I won't say no to that," I said with a flirty laugh, adding the next charm to the chain.

I opened the final box and found a handful of charms inside. I pulled my brows together, wondering why he had given me the others one at a time, but these were all together.

"Those are for you to add to your bracelet as you go. Whatever path you take in life, there's a charm to help guide you."

I studied them in my hands and smiled when I saw one that was a house and a few that were pets, including cats and dogs. There was a palm tree and sunshine, probably in case I decided to move somewhere warm and sunny. Then there were some that reminded me of Sugarplum Falls and the beautiful Christmas-obsessed town that was starting to grow on me.

I grabbed the coffee charm and added it to the chain.

"I think Sam's lattes deserve a special place on this bracelet," I said, feeling my throat burn from the tears I didn't want to shed.

"It's whatever you want it to be, Brynlee. Whatever life *you* choose."

I looked down at the couple kissing and held the charm between my fingers as I studied it. I wanted to choose Sebastian and a future together, but deep down, it scared the shit out of me. No one had stayed in my life long enough for me to love, so why would now be any different?

Thirty
Sebastian

This morning with Brynlee had been great, but I was a little surprised when she told me she wanted to go to her aunt's for dinner. When she mentioned that she wanted to go over early, I became more concerned that it wasn't just about spending time with them. It was to spend time with them before she left for good.

We pulled into the driveway and parked, Brynlee fidgeting in her seat the entire drive over. She unbuckled and hopped out of the truck before I could go around and open her door for her.

"What's going on?" I asked quietly, shoving my hands into my pockets as she rang the doorbell.

"Nothing. Why?"

I could hear the lie in her voice and hated it.

"Because I know you well enough by now to know that something is going on. Are we here because you want to spend time with your family on Christmas, or are we here so you can say goodb—"

"Hello!" Beth greeted, the door flying open as she extended her arms to hug her niece.

"Hi, Aunt Beth," Brynlee said, her arms wrapped around her.

Once they were done, Beth pulled me in for a hug and then stepped aside to let us in.

"Um, actually, I need to talk to Brynlee real quick," I interjected, grabbing her arm to keep her from going inside.

Her eyes widened as she stared at me, but her aunt didn't seem bothered by it.

"Of course. Just come inside when you're ready. I've got a pot of hot chocolate ready, and Hadley is going through the board games." She smiled and then shut the door, giving us some privacy.

"What was that?" Brynlee asked, her whisper just below a shriek.

"We're not going in there until I know what's going on with you. You've been acting weird since last night, and I can't help but feel like you're pulling away. So I'm going to ask again—what's going on?"

She shook her head and folded her arms over her chest.

"I can't do this. Okay? Is that what you wanted to hear?"

"If it's the truth, then yes."

"Fine. You've got your answer. Now, can we please go inside? It's freezing out here, and I don't want to lose more time with them."

"Bryn—"

"No." She raised her hand and stopped me. "I don't know what the future holds for me, Sebastian. But I know I've been let down more times than I can count, and I refuse to let myself get attached to something that might not last either."

I tipped my head back and tried to calm myself, but before I could talk to her, she was opening the door and heading inside.

******

The day carried on with everyone being pleasant and playing games, but we could all feel the tension in the room from words that went unspoken. By dinner time, I felt like I wanted to ram my head into the wall from the frustration I felt with Brynlee shutting down and pushing everyone out. I could tell by the concerned looks exchanged between her aunt and cousin that they also knew something was going on.

We retreated to the living room after we cleaned up dinner and sat on the plump couches. I noticed Brynlee's foot tapping anxiously on the rug as she looked up at the clock on the wall more times than I could count.

"So, what are your guys' plans for New Year's Eve?" Beth asked nonchalantly, folding her hands in her lap as she looked at us.

"*Mom*," Hadley hissed through her teeth in warning.

"What? It's obvious something is going on, and I wouldn't be me if I didn't try to figure it out. My guess is now that the storm is passing, they're stuck figuring out what's next. You can't blame me for being curious about what that means for us and our relationship with Brynlee. I lost her once, so I'm not letting her go this time without a fight."

I turned and looked at Brynlee, noticing the heat flaming her cheeks.

"I'd like to know, too. We keep saying we're going to talk about it, but then we don't."

"I told you, I can't do this," she said quietly, avoiding looking at her family. "Please don't push me right now."

"I kinda feel like I have to," I admitted with a frustrated sigh. "I don't want to wake up tomorrow and you're gone. That's what this feels like, and I don't like it. I've already told you I will go wherever you go, Brynlee. You don't have to worry about that. Just let me be a part of whatever this is."

"Are you planning to leave Sugarplum Falls?" Hadley asked, looking directly at Brynlee.

She nodded and brushed the tear away as it slid down her cheek.

"Where will you go?" Beth questioned. "We don't even know where home is for you. There's so much I want to know about you, Brynlee."

"Home is in Oregon. But it's never felt like it. This was just supposed to be a week away so I could lock myself in a hotel room and get my book done. I couldn't focus back home and thought maybe if I got away for a while, I would find—"

"Yourself?" I offered softly. "You did find yourself, Brynlee. You found more than that. You found your family. You found me."

"But none of that was supposed to happen!" She stood up and started pacing in front of the tree.

"Fate is funny that way," I laughed. "I wasn't sure where I was going, but I'm glad I got stuck here because being with you feels like anything *but* being stuck. I was trying to find myself, too, Brynlee. And I found you. Nothing has ever felt more meant to be in my life. Ever."

"But don't you get it? This is all happening too soon! Everything is happening at once, and I'm forced to make all of these decisions, and I don't know what to do! I've barely known you for twelve days, Sebastian. Twelve days!"

I stood up and stepped in front of her to stop her from pacing. I reached for her hands and gently held them in mine.

"What difference does it make if it's twelve days or twelve months? Twelve months or twelve years?" My eyes begged her to hear my words and trust that they came straight from my heart. "Love has to start somewhere, Brynlee. And for me, it started twelve days ago."

"It makes a lot of difference for someone like me who has *never* had anyone stick around that long. I would be lying if I said I wasn't petrified of you deciding this wasn't worth it and having you up and leave me. I can't stand the thought of being abandoned by anyone else, Sebastian. So yeah, maybe this is the coward way out, but I'm protecting myself by not letting anything happen in the first place."

"How else am I going to prove to you that I won't do that to you if you don't give me a chance to try?"

"That's a big risk. It may not mean as much to you, but there's a lot on the line for me with this. I've had my heart broken so many times over the years that I worry one more little break will be the one to shatter it completely," she whispered, dropping her head.

Without thinking it through, I dropped onto my knee and stared at her.

"I don't have a ring because I wasn't planning to do this today. But trust me, Brynlee, I'm not afraid to do this.

There's nothing that will stand in my way of being with you. My heart found the person I'm meant to be with, and I will not easily give that up. So marry me. Let me make those vows to you that I will be there for you. Through thick and thin. Sickness and health. All of it, Brynlee. Marry me."

I heard her aunt and cousin gasp but kept my eyes locked on Brynlee's.

"Marry me. Be my wife, and let me show you how my love for you is never-ending, Brynlee. Let me heal the parts of you that are broken. Let me love you the way you deserve to be loved. Spend your life with me, and let me show you happily ever after."

"That's not how this works," she whispered, her features softening. "I know you're a true romantic at heart because of what you write, but this is real life, Sebastian. This isn't a fictional story where they are given whatever they want and live happily ever after."

"Sure it is."

She tilted her head and frowned at me.

"Our meet-cute was at the hotel. We were then thrown into forced proximity with a cabin with only one bed. Then, we quickly became strangers to lovers. We're stranded in a small town. I'm obviously an adorable cinnamon roll hero, and you're an independent heroine who doesn't need anyone to rescue her. Our chemistry is intense, and our sex is more explicit than some of the stuff I write about. So yeah, Brynlee, our love story is a true romance. And we will have our happily ever after."

"I guess it's better than if I had written the story," she joked, her cheeks flushing after I admitted how hot our sex life was.

"True. That would have had a different ending, and I'm sure you would have had me as the villain who stalked and tried to murder you before you outwitted me and took me down."

"It's a kill-or-be-killed world," she said with a grin.

"My knee is starting to hurt, so do you think you can agree to marry me so I can get up."

"I don't know. Maybe I should go for someone younger. Someone with better knees." She scrunched her face.

"I'm only thirty-two, and while my knees are bad from playing high school football, you know the rest of me is just fine."

 I grabbed her wrist and pulled her down into me.

"I love you so much more than you could ever know. So, please put me out of my misery and spend the rest of my life with me. Marry me, Brynlee, because I don't want to spend another second of my life without you."

She looked from me to her aunt and cousin, who were watching intently from the couch.

"I love you too, Sebastian." A single tear slid down her cheek as she made my heart race by making me wait for an answer. "Yes, I'll marry you!"

Her cheeks split into a grin as I wrapped my hand around the back of her head and brought my lips to hers.

"You just gave me the best gift ever," I whispered once we came up for air.

"Better than the gloves?"

"A thousand times better. I'm going to make you the happiest woman in the world, baby," I promised.

"We still have to figure out what's next. Home is Oregon for me, but I don't want to force you to move there."

"I told you, I'll go wherever you want me to. If you love Oregon, that's where we'll live."

"I don't. That's the problem," she sighed, pulling my hand as I stood up.

"Why not stay in Sugarplum Falls?" Beth suggested, her eyes wide with hope. "I know I'm probably overstepping, but it would be so wonderful to have you guys here. I missed so much of your life, Brynlee. I don't want to miss anymore."

Brynlee looked from her aunt then to me.

"What do you think?"

"I think we should start looking at houses in Sugarplum Falls."

"Me too," she said with a smile, wrapping her arms around my waist as I kissed her head. "I could definitely live here, especially with Sam's lattes and those truffles from Sugarplum Sweets."

"Well, lucky for you guys, my mom happens to own Sugarplum Realty," Hadley said, her face beaming with an ear-to-ear smile.

"I'm so happy you guys are staying," Beth said, coming over to hug us as Hadley joined in. "This truly is the best Christmas ever."

Epilogue
Brynlee
One Year Later

"I cannot believe that we have a booth at Frosty Fest," I said, helping Sebastian set up the banner behind our tables.

"I bet you didn't think you'd be cowriting with your husband either, but here we are."

"One of the best decisions I ever made."

He arched an eyebrow and stared at me.

"Besides buying a house in Sugarplum Falls and moving in with you."

His other eyebrow shot up, and he folded his arms over his chest.

"Okay, okay. Marrying you was probably the best thing that happened this year out of all of the other wonderful things."

I wrapped my arms around his neck and kissed him. But I wasn't lying. Marrying Sebastian was the best thing I had ever done. I never knew the happiness that could come from picking the perfect house together, but that joy was topped when Bert gave us the tree I'd fallen in love with at the cabin. We'd adorned it with the ornaments we bought last year, but this time, it was in our house, along with a million other decorations. It turned out that the residents of Sugarplum Falls weren't the only ones obsessed with Christmas these days.

"That's more like it, Mrs. Whitaker."

"Hey, hey, hey, keep all that stuff outta here," Hadley teased, getting to her booth a few minutes late. "Just because you're living your real-life romance doesn't mean the rest of us want to see it."

"Good morning, Had," I said, smiling at my cousin. "Do you need help setting up?"

"I think I'm good. A few people from the store should be here soon to help. But I do need to get a copy of the book and have both of you sign it."

"We already took care of it," Sebastian answered. "Assume your stocking has been stuffed."

"I'd rather it was something else getting stuffed," she muttered, only loud enough for me to hear.

"What happened with that guy your mom set you up with?" I asked, handing Sebastian a stack of books from the box to set out on the table.

"The new realtor? Ugh, he's so pompous and arrogant. I can't stand him."

"Do I smell an enemies to lovers romance blooming?" Sebastian teased, ducking as Hadley threw a stocking at him.

The other employees from Sugarplum Gifts showed up and helped Hadley set up while I grabbed more books and arranged them on the other end of the table.

After both of us finished the series we had been working on, we decided to take a break and created a romantic suspense pen name. It turned out that I had been able to work faster when I had someone to sprint with, which allowed me to finish the last three books in my series ahead of schedule. It was perfect timing that we both completed our other projects at the same time so we could embark on a new journey together.

With our new books, I handled all the suspense parts while Sebastian made them hot and steamy on the romance side. It gave both of us a much needed change, and we learned that writing together was more fun than writing on our own.

We went back and forth on what pen name to use, then finally decided on S.B. Whitaker when I pointed out that B.S. Whitaker sounded like we were full of shit. Our first book was released around Thanksgiving and sold like hotcakes. When our agent asked if we would be willing to do a book signing, Sebastian agreed, but only if it was in Sugarplum Falls. That created such a massive response that the two hotels in town had sold out within minutes.

"Are you ready for this?" I asked Sebastian, knowing he was nervous about his first signing. After word got out about who the real F.E. Tish was, pictures started circulating about America's hottest romance author. When we decided to start our new penname, we both agreed that we weren't going to keep our identities hidden. I'd spent so much of my life not knowing who I was that I didn't want to hide it another minute.

"As long as I have you by my side, I'm ready for anything."

He reached for my hand and held it, the charms on my bracelet catching the light. We both smiled as we looked down at the one of a baby tucked in between the house and the married couple charms. Life had been a wild ride over the past year, but I couldn't wait to see what our future held. In six months, we would be welcoming a new baby, and I knew it would be the most loved baby in the world.

****

Ready for more Sugarplum Falls? Be sure to check out the other novellas in this series.

Blame It On The Mistletoe

https://books2read.com/u/bw1rqe

Blame It On The Eggnog

https://books2read.com/u/38PPY6

Blame It On The Candy Canes

https://books2read.com/u/31DNo7

Don't forget to grab your free holiday novella, A Very Merry Kissmas! https://dl.bookfunnel.com/xb0vx4j6kk

Other Books By Samantha Baca

The Haven Brook Series (small-town romantic suspense):

'Til Death Do Us Part (Haven Brook Book 1)

https://books2read.com/u/m2RJNR

The Cradle Will Fall (Haven Brook Book 2)

https://books2read.com/u/b6O0QE

The Ties That Bind (Haven Brook Book 3)

https://books2read.com/u/mqgoz8

A Very Haven Christmas (Haven Brook Book 4- Novella)

https://books2read.com/u/mvqGjj

Three Strikes, You're Gone (Haven Brook Book 5)

https://books2read.com/u/mvqL2z

The Dark Shadows Trilogy
(romantic suspense)

Five Steps Ahead (Dark Shadows Book 1)

https://books2read.com/u/38Q0gO

Ten Seconds Too Late (Dark Shadows Book 2)

https://books2read.com/u/3JRgVB

Against The Clock (Dark Shadows Book 3)

https://books2read.com/u/m2YwoR

The Stone Creek Series
(small-town- novellas)

Chocolate Covered Mistletoe (Stone Creek Book 1)

https://books2read.com/u/3LRk9N

Candy Coated Promises (Stone Creek Book 2)

https://books2read.com/u/mldP5Y

Pumpkin Spiced Possibilities (Stone Creek Book 3)

https://books2read.com/u/bojdwV

<u>Beaumont Creek Series</u>
<u>(small town)</u>

Just One Time (Beaumont Creek Book 1)

https://books2read.com/u/3G52zK

Second Chances (Beaumont Creek Book 2)

https://books2read.com/u/4Aj6Z0

Third Time's The Charm (Beaumont Creek Book 3)

https://books2read.com/u/b5lEyG

Four-ever Single (Beaumont Creek Book 4)

https://books2read.com/u/4j5jMX

Fifth Wheel (Beaumont Creek Book 5)

https://books2read.com/u/4XwKwa

<u>Whiskey Mountain Series</u>
<u>(small-town- novellas)</u>

Something To Talk About

https://books2read.com/u/4X62ag

Something To Think About

https://books2read.com/u/3GWAan

Something To Believe In

https://books2read.com/u/3yVzgB

Something To Live For

https://books2read.com/u/mllEOP

<u>Sugarplum Falls Series</u>
<u>(Holiday Novellas- can be read as standalone)</u>

Blame It On The Mistletoe

https://books2read.com/u/bw1rqe

Blame It On The Eggnog

https://books2read.com/u/38PPY6

Blame It On The Candy Canes

https://books2read.com/u/31DNo7

Blame It On The Blizzard

https://books2read.com/u/b6z6XE

<u>Standalone Books</u>

One Last Wish

https://books2read.com/u/mqg7D9

Finding Love In Apartment 2C (novella)

https://books2read.com/u/bze9aZ

Cocky Counsel: A Hero Club Novel

https://books2read.com/u/31Kzkn

All Is Fair In Food And War (novella)

https://books2read.com/u/bp8qjX

<u>Holiday Books</u>

<u>(novellas)</u>

Snow Place To Go

https://books2read.com/u/4A560N

A Christmas Wish

https://books2read.com/u/4EKXpE

Holiday Hijinks

https://books2read.com/u/4DP6Ze

Acknowledgments

When I first started writing books back in 2020, I never imagined I would be finishing my 28th book at the end of 2023. It's been such a fun and amazing journey! Thank you for coming along with me and for reading Blame It On The Blizzard. I hope you enjoyed the story as much as I loved writing it!

Amanda—I know I have thanked you a hundred times already for everything you do for me, but I don't plan to stop any time soon. You're an amazing friend, and I'm so thankful to have you as an alpha reader. Thank you for talking through ideas with me and helping me problem-solve when I need it. I truly appreciate your friendship and look forward to the future books we'll work on together!

Claire, Valerie, Jackie, and Malissa—thank you for your constant support and help with beta reading this book for me. I love the feedback you provide and how you all have learned my style so well that you know what things will bother me when I miss them. You keep me on my toes, and it's so appreciated! Thank you for everything you ladies do!

Thank you to Natasha for reading this in ONE DAY when I reached out and asked for a very last-minute read-through to ensure we had caught everything in the initial rounds of editing. I appreciate your feedback and how much you love this series!

To my parents and sister—thank you for your constant support and for telling everyone you meet about how I write books and where to find them. I love you guys!

Richard—you are my real-life cinnamon roll hero, always stepping in to save the day and helping me to meet deadlines. I will never stop appreciating everything you do for me. From helping with book covers to attending signings with me, I'm so thankful for your support with all of my book stuff. I love you so much!

To my girls—I will never stop pushing you to go after what you want in life. There will always be challenges, but you're strong enough to overcome them. Dream big and reach for those stars. The world is yours, and I cannot wait to see where you go.

I want to thank my ARC readers who grabbed this one and were so quick to leave a review! I can't tell you how many times I had to add more copies on BookSirens because the demand for this story was so high! Thank you for loving my books enough that you jumped on the ARC for this one as soon as you saw it. I appreciate you so much!

About the Author

Samantha lives in the southwest with her husband and two small children after abandoning her childhood dream of living in a cabin in Colorado when she found that she couldn't afford to live there and was deathly allergic to the woods. When she's not writing, she's usually spouting off sarcastic remarks while drinking wine out of a coffee mug to look like a functional adult while chasing down her toddlers. She enjoys spending time with her family, watching reruns of Friends, and the 24/7 flow of coffee that can be found in her veins. Be sure to follow her on social media for updates on what she's working on.

You can find her here:

Facebook: https://www.facebook.com/AuthorSamanthaBaca

Instagram: https://instagram.com/author_samantha_baca

Goodreads: http://www.goodreads.com/authorsamanthabaca

Facebook Reader Group:https://www.facebook.com/groups/2945710968775398/

Webpage: https://authorsamanthabaca.wordpress.com

Newsletter: http://eepurl.com/g0NcSj